FAREWELL
TO THE ANCIENT GODS

"A godling, with little tasks to do. What
a time they've had, they and the gods of the
countryside. The Christians cursing them at
every chance and taking them for demons
out of Hell. No one except the country folk
to bring them offerings of milk and honey
combs. Roads and cities blackening their
fields. Altars overgrown with tanglewood.
Sacred images becoming dolls for girls to
drop and trample underfoot. Except perhaps
the bees, who have always been their friends.
You say they've gone, the Sprites?"

"Fled to the distant north. To hide in
caves and woods, and well for *us*."

G. Barr

THE GODS ABIDE

Thomas Burnett Swann

Illustrated by
George Barr

DAW BOOKS, INC.

DONALD A. WOLLHEIM, PUBLISHER

1301 Avenue of the Americas
New York, N.Y.   10019

Cover art by George Barr

Dedication

To Pam,
who is Stella,
golden among the goddesses

FIRST PRINTING, DECEMBER 1976

1 2 3 4 5 6 7 8 9

PRINTED IN U.S.A.

Prologue

He watched the little workers carrying olive leaves which, vessel-like, cupped feasts of honey in their holds. He laughed and seized a leaf and spread his other hand to tempt the bees and show his gratitude.

"Poor little giant," they seemed to buzz. "Forgotten in our fields. Trust to us for food."

Late summer rested lightly on the land: Grapes like empurpled honey combs athwart the vines, awaiting slaves to pluck them, tread them, singing harvest songs. Hillocks, earth's own breasts. A friendly serpent of a river coiled as if to inundate the fields. Olive trees, a rustling silver fleece; and to the south, a golden fleece of barley, rye, and wheat to tempt an Argonaut. A summer house, brick roof and blue-framed door, where slaves could eat and rest and, resting now beneath the noonday sun, left human-silent fields to bees—and him.

The north? Beyond the town, the hillocks rose to sandstone hills; brushwood instead of wheat. Russet instead of green. He did not like the North.

He sensed before he saw his visitors. The sound of bees had masked their sandaled feet, the man-tall wheat had hidden their approach. Robes like winding sheets encompassed them as if against the sun (or taint of sin?).

"Naked," frowned the man. He might have said "barbaric" or "demoniac."

"He's only a baby," said the woman, with quiet reproof.

"A fat five, I'd say. Call that a baby?"

"Plump, not fat." Then, turning from the frown. "Who are you, golden boy?"

"No-do-tus," he said, proud to make the syllables appear a proper name and not an infant's gibberish. Magic lived in names as in a Sibyl's cave or Dyrad's tree. (The

5

cave might be untenanted, the tree without a green-haired girl; the meaning of the name become obscure; still, magic abided under many masks.)

"Nodotus," mused the woman. " 'Helper of the Stalks.' Named for a corn Sprite in the oldest cult. Hair as gold as corn to suit a Sprite. I am Marcia. This Marcus, my husband."

"Such Sprites were phallic, weren't they?" scowled the man. "Well, they're gone. It's Christ and Mithras now."

"And gentle Isis."

"For you women folk. At any rate, the name won't do." His eyes held iron and slashes marred his brow. He seemed to have been made for war; he captained triremes for the Emperor; fought battles; won and lost; somehow survived; grew hard instead of wise; and kept his wounds like laurel leaves to symbolize his fight.

Not that little boys could notice such details. Nodotus thought of nothing more precise than Gloom.

"We shall call him Nod for short," the woman said. "Nod, how old are you?"

"Don't know." Indeed, he did not even know how he had come into the field. He only knew that he had come to like the woman and dislike the man. Perhaps she had a taste for honied leaves. "Here." She took his gift as if it were an emperor's dish, the udder of a sow in tunny sauce, snails on asparagus, and licked the green and living platelet of its sweet.

"About how old?"

"Five," he said, remembering Marcus' guess.

She turned to Marcus with a smile to melt his iron. "You see? It's as if he knows, well, more than he has said. Or learns as fast as you and I. As if he understands."

"Understands? I'd say he was half asleep. He's only moved to offer you a leaf. At least you've named him well. Nod."

"He isn't indolent, my dear. It's simply that he economizes when he moves."

"Most economical brat I ever saw."

"Marcus, we shall have to take him home with us. He's

not from the town, that's for sure." The town was Misna, Etruscan-built but sacked by Gauls and later occupied by Romans from the south. "Not with that yellow hair. I think—I think—he may be what his name implies."

"A *real* Sprite?" He spoke with more distaste than disbelief. Such Sprites had frolicked in the forests of the Golden Age. Godlings, demi-gods, beast-men—the many names were one.

"A godling, with little tasks to do. What a time they've had, they and the gods of the countryside. The Christians cursing them at every chance and taking them for demons out of Hell." (Had she misplaced her smile on such a sunny day, and after finding *him*?) "No one except the country folk to bring them offerings of milk and honey combs. Roads and cities blackening their fields. Altars overgrown with tanglewood. Sacred images becoming dolls for girls to drop and trample underfoot." Wistfully she watched the swarm departing from the field, an onyx cloud to her, no doubt; a saffron cloud to Nod, who saw with more than eyes. "Except perhaps the bees, who have always been their friends. You say they've gone, the Sprites?"

"Fled to the distant north. To hide in caves and woods, and well for *us*."

"Might Nod have been forgotten in the flight? Or hidden in the fields he knew—and stayed? You'll note the stubborn chin. He looks like one accustomed to his way."

"If he was overlooked, it was deliberate. I have no doubts he was a mischievous spirit, a prankster and a thief."

"At *five?*"

"You said yourself he has an older air. With Sprites, who can say? Always in trouble, a scourge to his mother, a curse to his father, and better left in the fields. And you would have him in our house? Why, the place is centuries old, and who can say what Sprites and Demons still remain? You'd add another such?" In early times, a "demon" had belonged between immortal gods and mortal men. The growing cult of Christ reserved the term for evil beings leagued with Satan and his thirst for human souls.

"If Nod is a corn Sprite, he will bring us luck. They did in the old days at any rate. The nurtured the wheat and saved it from drouth and the red mildew. Sometimes they followed you about to keep you out of harm and left you tiny gifts of food and flowers."

"Suppose he's just a human boy?"

"Well, we could use a child about the place. He looks a sturdy chap. He hasn't cried or frowned, what with being abandoned and hungry—"

"The bees fed him."

"And happened upon by you and me, who must appear to him like Cyclopes, all huge and gray and loud. His disposition is unquestionably excellent. Give him a few more years and he can help us in the house."

"We have three slaves."

"And used to have seven. Later, he can oversee your fields. That manager of yours bears watching. Especially when you go to sea."

"I am quite capable of watching my manager without the help of a so-called corn Sprite. If he is what you say, he'll pluck the choicest sprays and eat them like sausages. Furthermore," he added, as if to clench his argument— clenched fists, clenched arguments, they suited him— "you know how babies are. Destructive. He'll soil our couch. You'll have to sew him robes—loin cloths— whatever babies wear—he'll soil them too. I doubt he's ever seen a water closet."

"My dear, housebreaking a baby is not beyond my skills, and I strongly suspect that this baby is already housebroken, or treebroken, or whatever it is that corn Sprites live in."

"*Am*," said Nod.

"If not destructive, expensive. Have you considered what he will cost to feed? Look at those fat cheeks." (It did not seem to Nod a time to kick or bite; not with a mother and a home at stake.)

"Considerably less than a slave who toils in your

vineyard. And one thing is certain. If we leave him now, he'll starve—or worse."

"The bees will feed him."

"You said that once. The bees die in winter."

The bees die in winter.... Cruel, cruel, thought Nod, for them—and me. (At five or thereabouts, it was not easy to forego the "me.") He tried to look alert, constructive, clean, and knowledgeable about—what was the word?—water closets, which he took to be a sort of storage tank.

"Plump. Pomegranate-cheeked," continued Marcus, as if he were reciting sins for which a man might be consigned to Hell. "Hair enough for several heads. And *yellow*. All that honey, I should think. I could swear he called the bees to him."

"Well, corn Sprites do. But even they are helpless with the wolves. This is the north, you know. Wolves and griffins too."

"Someone else will doubtless find him. Farmers come this way. That summer house—"

"Dusil, if not wolves. Red-haired imps with foxes' tails. *Phallic*."

A grunt of acquiescence.

She scooped him into arms which seemed expressly made to hold, caress, protect—she did not seem to mind his sticky hands—and strode ahead of Marcus toward the town. The grayness of her suddenly seemed to shine.

"Oh, very well," he muttered, overtaking her and reasserting his authority (or so he thought; Nod saw her smile).

"Marcus, he has given me a gift already! A bunch of violets. He must have hidden them in his fist."

"They're crushed."

"I like them anyway." She spread the mangled blossoms in her hand and sniffed them lovingly, as if they were Hispanian hyacinths.

In later years, he sometimes wished that he had been forsaken to the wolves.

Part I:
JOININGS

★ Chapter One ★

He dozed among the leathery holothurians—he, Dylan, 'Son of the waves—resting his head on a jelly fish, the frigid water above him a wall instead of a weight, a concealment instead of a drowning. The currents were often swift and tumultuous: Roman warships and Celtic coracles rounded this coast of Caledonia rarely and at their risk. The beaches were littered with bleached and broken coral from the murderous sea; bitter sea-grapes rose into hills or *braes* where one leafless oak, contorted by lightning and wind, stood like a bent old leper. Even the Saxon pirates across the channel avoided this land to the north of Britannia, this land of Scoti. There was nothing to steal.

Like a dolphin, however, he never slept soundly or long; like a dolphin or seal, he must watch for vicious Shelleycoats, who revealed their approach with a clatter of sea-shells caught in their smothering flippers, and silent Merrows from Eire, always curious, always ready to trick, steal, or kill.

He woke with a start; he woke to a difference. He felt a movement of waters and not a natural current. An object had passed above him, blotting the light of the sun. A whale? His sensitive nostrils quivered for blubber but wrinkled with wood and tar. A ship? He did not hear the slap of a trireme. A merchantman then; sails instead of oars. Not that a merchant could find any wealth in this region. Still, the Romans were always in search of tin. He could have told them that they must look to the south, or so he supposed, for to him the south was treasure: animals, friends, forests dimly recalled as if from an earlier life (in fact from an earlier life?).

Why not tell them before they wasted a summer or floundered on hidden shoals? Talk to them in his rusty

Latin and the words remembered from another and nameless tongue? Of storms and monsters and Saxon raiders, whose ships were called the Reindeer of the Sea but resembled dragons with bristling teeth? Of faraway Rome, the city of marble, and nearer Londinium, the city of brick? Just to talk and be answered with words instead of the curlew's melancholy wail; the well-intentioned but incomprehensible rasp of Angus, his six-legged friend! Just to break bread and pour libations of wine to whatever gods of the sea could protect a mariner exiled from home or a boy who did not know his home! How many summers since a Roman ship had wrecked on the beach and he had befriended the crew, helped them repair a raked and battered hull and a broken mast, and learned the rudiments of Latin in time to wish them an "ave atque vale"? Forsaken before the coming of the Romans, his past as blank as a clean palimpsest, he had worked and learned and watched the sea for another ship; he has survived. He had not, however, made friends with loneliness, that bogle which slept in the day but emerged at night to taunt him with mists of memory and expectation.

Disentangling himself from his watery bed, he shot to the surface, gills quiescent and closed, lungs gulping air. Amphibious, he could breathe with equal facility under or out of the water, but quick transitions sometimes choked or dizzied him. In the past, the Romans had been his friend. He shook the shells from his hair, waved his hand, and shouted in his best remembered Latin:

"Ship ahoo!" (Or was it "ahoy?")

His heart leapt in his breast like a mackerel on a hook. Had they returned to him, his friends of that friendly summer? A wingéd whale, he thought. A Pegasus gliding through the waves. Then, turning practical, he assessed the ship with a keen nautical eye:

A large merchantman with tilted stern and prow, each surrounded by a low gallery; mainsail and foresail brailed and divided into squares; wicker deckhouse humped at the stern, like a beehive chopped in half, its open side protected by canvas hangings.

It was not the same ship. It was neither so large, nor

clean, nor—here the impractical dreamer in him supplied the word—bonny. It was neither a wingéd whale nor a gliding Pegasus. *More like a pelican peerin' about for fish.*

He confronted wood and tar and canvas, and dirty men in such a variety of garments—tunics, cloaks, sheepskins—that he could not distinguish the captain from his officers, or the officers from the men. Had the ship not borne the eagle standard of Rome, he might have taken her for a pirate's prize.

The vessel had passed directly above him and moved toward the land and an intervening shoal. He overtook her and shouted to those on the deck:

"Name's Dylan. Change course. Starboard. *Quick.*"

Quick was slow for the pilot, but not too slow to escape what Dylan liked to call the Jawbone of the Sea.

Sailors gathered along the deck and stared at him with a mixture of curiosity and fear. He knew that the Romans hated the sea, particularly beyond the Pillars of Hercules and their own Māre Nostrum with its pharos and fortresses. They always expected storms and carnivorous Sirens, Merrows and Shellycoats.

He leaped completely out of the water to show his shape.

"See!" he cried. "Sealskin's borrowed. Not a flick o' fin or tail."

"Christ, it's a naked boy," cried a fat, one-eared chap who appeared to be the captain from the boom in his voice. He had the look of a walrus, the squat body, the lack of a neck. He had the fishy stench.

"Looks like a Triton to me," said a small, stoat-like fellow, scraggly-blond, Celtic, hair crisp with salt winds and the need to wash.

"No tail."

"What do I need wi' a tail?" cried Dylan with growing impatience. He had thought that the *lack* of a tail would reassure his guests.

"Sealskin cloak though," observed the Walrus. "Ain't human. That's for sure. Must be a Roane. Notice how quick he overtook us? Quicker than a dolphin. And the gills. That's how he breathes under water." He pointed rudely at the narrow, almost invisible slits in Dylan's sides. "And the webbed toes. Lord! Must've angered up Neptune. Sent us a storm he did, the grouchy old god. Ought to be in the Channel. Sent us here to *him*."

"And you a Christian?" The Stoat cawed like a gull gloating over a fish.

"Old Ones still about. Making mischief. Like him. What'd you say he was? Demon for sure."

"Roane. Never met one before. Heard though. Folk say they're a friendly race. Kind to strangers. Domestic. Love the babies—bairns to them. Always a-building. Live in coracles roofed with reeds. Fish for a livelihood. Stay close to home. But if you make one mad, *watch out*. Strong as a Cyclops. Teeth like a bear trap."

"Goin' to invite me aboard?" He was not in the least cold, he was never cold. But he wanted a conversation which included *him*. He could have told them at once that he was hospitable, unless compelled to tread water while strangers discussed him like a slave on the block.

A skinny rope ladder slithered into the water. A sick snake, he thought.

"Dinna need *that*," said Dylan, who sprang with a flourish of show-manship onto the deck. (Before he finished his show, they would wish themselves into Roanes—gills, webbed feet, sealskin cloak; in a word, agility.)

The Captain looked at him with surprise and disapproval. "Don't have a tunic, boy?"

"No need. Never get cold."

"Loin cloth?"

"Slow me down in the water."

"But what about that skin around your shoulders?"

"Not the same. Gives me a lift in the water. Speed too."

"Roane all right," muttered Stoat. "A conjured skin or I miss my guess."

Brazenly the Captain fingered Dylan's arm. The gesture was curious, not paternal.

"Slick," he said.

"Like a—what-do-you-call-it—seal," Dylan explained,

struggling with his rudimentary Latin. "Eases me through the waves. Dries in a whisk o' wind."

"Ought to wear a tunic," said the Captain. "Naked like that. And a boy your age. A big fourteen, I'd say."

"Might make a lusty stud," whispered Stoat. "Equipped, if you see what I mean."

Stud? The word was new to Dylan. Naked? They must have forgotten his cloak. "Shoulders ain't naked. What's to worry? Age? Never kept count. Fourteen 'ull do."

A shrug and a mutter. Well, the Romans had always made a show of decorum, but why it was needful to wear a garment around your loins, he did not pretend to know.

The Captain gave his arm a hurtful pinch. "Good muscles. All that swimming, eh? Other tricks can be learnt in a hurry."

Dylan removed the Captain's hand with a sudden shrug and brushed the hair from his eyes for a better look at the first man he had ever wanted to hit. *Eyes too squinty for the big head. Fat like a walrus; whiskers too. Acts like a Merrow. Watch 'im, Dylan. May want to steal your skin.*

"Well favored too," Stoat added, as if to apologize for his captain's crudity. Well favored? Dylan had never owned a looking glass. He had seen his reflection in tide pools and taken it as a matter of course that his hair was as black as onyx, as soft as heather; his eyes the blue of lapis lazuli from an ocean cave; his mouth forever ready to curve into a smile; his teeth as white and perfect as pearls extracted by Sirens from oysters to wear in their silver tresses. At least he did not resemble the Walrus or the Stoat.

Dylan's only acquaintance with Romans had been the time when the merchantman had run aground in a storm and its crew had camped on the beach through the summer, he bringing them fish and rowan berries, they teaching him sailor's Latin and training Angus in the use of their tools. He had liked them. He trusted strangers. Except, now, the Walrus and the Stoat.

He felt ashamed of mistrust. He felt the jellyfish stings of remorse. The men had done him no wrong. They had

asked him aboard their ship. He must return and surpass
the invitation. It was his code. It was one of the shards
from his forgotten past.

"Care to bide wi' me overnight, brithers? Have a cot on
the beach."

"Cot? Hammock, you mean. We've enough of those on
the ship."

"Hut, not hammock."

"Got a girlfriend hid away?"

"A jo? Nay." He had never seen a girl. Even the wan-
ton Sirens kept to warmer waters.

"What's the use of 'em?" he had asked those earlier
Romans.

"Your mother was one."

"Oh? That's where I come from is it?" (He did not
want a mother who left her son on a forsaken beach.)
What else they good for?"

"Fun."

"Like to swim races in the sea?"

"No."

"Fish?"

"No."

"Keep a man company wi' lively talk?"

"No."

"Ain't good for much 'sides a lot of no's, are they?"

The Romans had smiled a conspiratorial smile. "You'll
see."

Walrus and Stoat exchanged glances which Dylan inter-
preted to mean, "If you haven't a jo, can we bring the
crew?"

"No room," he hurried to add. (All of those dirty
sailors tramping through his cot? Their own ship, their
own cot, as it were, was an inexcusable mess. Decks
needed swabbing, hull needed tarring. Untidiest vessel he
had ever seen. Even the captain had lost the belt from his
tunic; perhaps his fat stomach had burst the catch. *What
is it the ship ain't? Ship-Shape, that's what. More like
ship-shoddy.* "Cot's a beached coracle. Small, don't you

see? Table sits *three*. Not much visitin' this far north. Ull
send the men some fish tomorrow."

The Captain looked unctuous, a walrus awaiting a
meal.

Dylan felt as if he had swallowed a live fiddler crab.
What was the name of the feeling? Mistrust compounded
with fear.

"Very well," said the Captain. He extended a hand,
amiable no doubt, but Dylan cringed as he felt the blub-
bery slab.

"Pilot, make for that point o' beach wi' the big black
rock. Clear channel all the way."

The pilot responded with a yawn and a lean on the
till. . . .

Dylan's cot, Dylan's coracle was permanently beached,
a permanent domicile. When he traveled, he preferred to
swim. It was a round-built boat of interwoven laths covered with painted canvas and domed with reeds and sun-
dried mud. In fact, it looked like a muddauber's nest, except for his special touches of color and comfort. If he
never thought of his own appearance, he prided himself
on his bonny home. He had set a door in the hull and
painted it with the color which the Druids used on their
bodies: (Instructions remembered from his Roman summer—dismember a woad plant, dry its parts, grind them
to pulp, and allow them to ferment into a paste which
produces a blue dye.) The rest of the hull was red—here,
the powdered roots of the madder had supplied him with
dye—and the sail, purely ornamental, was a beached and
spotless white. A bell and a lantern hung above the door.
He and Angus had built the cot with Roman tools; the
Romans, departing, had left him the lantern and bell.

Dylan rapped politely as if he were visiting somebody
else's house. A rasp and slither sounded behind the door,
which opened slowly, tentatively on its leathern hinges as
if it had a suspicious mind. A large black feeler waved in
the opening.

"Mars' holy shield, it's a Hydra head," cried the Stoat.

"Nothin' o' the sort," snapped Dylan. "It's Angus, and
he don't take to strangers."

"What under Jupiter's sky is the beast?" He might have been talking about a Sphinx.

"Ain't a beastie to me. Friend. Don't have a name 'sides Angus."

As large as a sheep dog, he was antlike in every other feature: six legs, many-faceted eyes, antennae which quivered like sprays of wheat in the wind. Dylan patted his bulbous head.

"Listens with them feelers," said Dylan. *"Those* feelers," he corrected himself, remembering his lessons in Latin from the earlier Romans.

"Hungry?" asked the Stoat, as if he would like to burrow under a hill.

"Course he's hungry. Been fishin'. Goin' to eat wi' us. Take off them dirty sandals and in we go."

"Going to eat *with* us?"

"What I said, didn't I?"

"Just wanted to make sure about the 'with.' "

The interior of the coracle was a single room, carpeted with fresh heather. It was also a clean and self-sufficient home, though Celtic in that it tempered order with spontaneity. Like a giant conch, it appeared to owe equally to Neptune's design and to its own individual whim: In the center, a table of roughly rounded cork. Three chairs. A bronze ewer for washing, set like a seat in a little chariot. To the side, a single hammock, closely meshed, suspended by iron hooks from the low ceiling. Below the hammock, a round, squashy cushion for Angus' bed.

The table was red and its feet were carved into wooden hippocampi. The chairs were blue, three-legged, their cushions lumpy with dried seaweed. A lantern—that is, a lamp enclosed in a wild goat's bladder—hung above the table. And Dylan had peopled the room with wooden companions. A naked girl. A seal with long whiskers and sleepy eyes. A Roman wearing a tunic. Finally, Dylan's special god, a bronze boy holding a bowl of patera and a spray of wheat—Bonus Eventus, the god of good luck.

"I'm a Christian," said Walrus, eying the pagan bronze.

"That's all right," Dylan agreed, "he dinna care."

"That naked girl. Where are her breasts?" asked Stoat.

"Mean chest? Got one just like mine."

"That's what I meant. Shouldn't have. She should—uh—bulge."

"Never saw a real lass," admitted Dylan. "Roman friend told me about 'em. Must o' left somethin' out. Bulge, ought she?"

"Twice."

"Up and down or side by side?"

"Side by side."

"Angus and me 'ull fix that. Anythin' else wrong? Sleekit enough below?"

"Passable. Doesn't have what she ought'nt to have."

"Glad about that. Bulge, eh? Makes a difference, don't it? Sort o' like ant hills."

"More like melons."

"Don't grow none hereabouts."

"That figures."

"What about that, Angus? Think we can come up wi' a couple o' ant hills, so to speak? Side by side?"

Angus replied with a frantic flurry of feelers.

"Like the thought, do you? So do I. It'll give her a sort o' surprise."

"Any Scoti in these parts?" questioned the Walrus.

Dylan preferred to talk about ant hills. "*Nobody* in these parts," he said testily, " 'cept what you see."

"Why the Hell do you stay?"

("Hell": the Christian word for the pagan Underworld. Worse, though. No Elysian Fields. *Hot.*) "Canna say." It was an honest answer. There was nothing to hold him on this barren coast except the inexplicable and irresistible need to wait for what he could not predict, for a time which he could not foretell. "Just bidin', I guess. Now to supper. What'll it be? Raw herrin' and plover eggs? Fish eye puddin'? Puts meat on the bones." Then, looking at Walrus, " 'Cept you don't need none."

"Haven't time," said Walrus with an abruptness which approached rudeness.

"Not to *sup*?" wailed Dylan. Never mind that he did not like the Walrus (ought to mind his manners), that he did not trust the Stoat (ought to bathe). They had failed

to compliment his house. Now they were about to depart
without partaking of his fare. He could not let them insult
his hospitality.

"Nope. Places to go."

"Got some rowan berry wine." He would allow them a
final chance. The black bat of anger fluttered uncomfort-
ably in his breast.

"Sounds good," said the Stoat, looking at the Walrus.
"Feel like that god o' yours when he hung on the cross."

"*Son* of God."

"Oh, thought he was somebody important."

"Said we haven't time."

"Well," said Dylan. "Suit yourselves. Eat wi' Angus
and me or go hungry." *Look down on me. They bein' human and Roman.* "Our Romans wasn't so particular."

Not only had they supped with him and taught him
Latin—ungrammatical to be sure, but practical—they had
complimented the house which their tools had helped him
to build. And not a man had reproached him for his lack
of memory, which except for his name stopped abruptly
around the age of eight, as if he had stepped from a
Caledonian mist, deep as midnight, into a pool of summer
sun. When they had questioned him about his past, he
had freely admitted the lack.

"Canna say. Hatched from a' egg like a turtle, maybe.
Who knows? Who cares? Might call me—what's the
word?—flotsam."

"Angus too?"

"Angus too."

He had deliberated for several days, debated within
himself, talked with the young man whose image he had
carved in wood.

"No," he had finally sighed. "Gotta bide here."

"What for?"

"Whatever left me here," he said, dimly groping in
memory. "Turtle or other, may come to fetch me."

Instead, a one-eared captain with a fat stomach and a
runt who needed a bath had come in a dirty ship, ignored
his house, refused his fare, and insulted his friend.

Dylan lifted a live mackerel from a pail of seawater and severed the head with his sharp teeth.

"See how good his teeth are?" said the Walrus to the Stoat.

"I maun live. Use 'em enough, don't I?"

"And that creature of yours—"

"Friend."

"A Telchin, I should think," said the Stout. "Used to have them in Italia. Pictures on old Etruscan walls. He can do things, can't he? I mean, with all those extra legs."

"Can't talk, but he sure as Hades can listen to folk who badmouth him. Better mind your tongue. He can be *mean*. Bites too."

"What else can he do?"

"Help out around the house. Sweep. Fish. Pick berries. Make a net. Company, too. Good listener, don't you see. Never talks back. Told you, he's my friend. Here, Angus, have a fish. Like herrin', mackerel better."

"Stow it," said the Walrus. "You'll both get a meal on the ship."

"Not comin' aboard till you sup wi' *me*. Wouldn't be meet."

"Come along now, boy. Don't make us knock out one of those pretty teeth. You'll lower your price. Our friends are waiting outside."

"Crew?"

Slavers. . . .

★ Chapter Two ★

Nod had gone to market for a gift (his mother had said, "Chrysanthemums would brighten this ancient house.") His arms abrim with flowers, he stayed but not to buy. For living flowers were far beyond his means. He stayed to watch them drive into the town, laughing, their plump, four-wheeled pilentum pulled by brawny mules. The wooden body of the wagon upreared an orange hood of many clothes; the mules' immaculately plaited tails swished rapid arcs to dislodge flies; innumerable bells rang silverly beneath the hood, and two young women waved to passersby and shook their braids like tassels in the wind.

"Corn Sprites," said a girl, ensconced behind a counter where earthen platters mingled with bronze goblets, amber beads, and fibulae of amethyst and sard. Her eyes, dark-ringed with kohl, her reddened mouth, announced a rarer ware than those her counter held. "Fleeing vengeful Christians, I should think. What with Constantine their friend, the Christians may start feeding *us* to lions."

"Harlots," sneered a man, a shepherd by his scent of dust and dung. The face above the sheepskin cloak looked harder than an adze. "Exiled from the south and seeking beds—and trade."

"Perhaps they carry beds beneath the hood," said Nod, enthusiastic; imagining the style of coverlit, the color of the cushions, most of all, the occupants without their robes or stolas. He, being still a pagan, hoped that Kohl Eyes recognized a Sprite. He, being still a virgin—whisper the hateful word—hoped that Dust and Dung had guessed the sprightly ladies' occupation. A sin to hope? "Earthly delights should be despised": thus his newly baptized father liked to preach. Nod's own conversion, though, was much in doubt. Fifteen, an aging virgin

24

uncommitted to the Ten Commandments, he would have
liked to sin before he asked forgiveness and renounced his
sinful ways. Fornication, lust, adultery ... forbidden
words ... intriguing words. ("Desire," a pagan would
have said, a compliment to women formed in Ceres',
Venus', Isis' sweet configuration.)

"My name is Stella," said the slimmer Sprite, miraculous with softnesses and laughter sweeter than her silver-
throated bells (the kind of miracle he much preferred to
multiplying loaves of bread or turning water into wine).
A spider must have spun her miracle of hair, extracting
bright from dark as if to plead, "I am my gift and not my
ugliness." Her scarlet stola matched her mouth, and yet
he could have sworn the mouth was not indebted to a carmine jar, a cosmetician's palette.

"I am Nod."

"And this is Tutelina, my belovéd friend."

Tutelina smiled and looked at Nod with invitation and
a silent truth: virginity is for the plain or dull. Her hair,
aside from its escaping yellow curls, was drawn into a
braid behind her back and bounced as freely as a sheep's
abortive tail; and he could read a slightly ovine look into
her rounded face. Buxom, yes. Bumptious, no. Mildly intelligent, mightily acquiscent with the proper ram. A win-
some bedmate for an inexperienced boy.

But not for him, since Stella filled his eye. And mind.
And heart, that organ shaped by Venus to incorporate her
stubborn, mystifying, and delightful will.

"Is there an inn?" asked Tuteline with her peacock-
feathered fan. Her voice reminded him of little girls solicit-
ing a honey cake or bunch of grapes. She asked as if she
did not dare expect a "Yes," and blinked her eyes to em-
phasize her plea.

"Sort of," he said. "But it's a sorry place, with dogs
and fleas. Even the rats look starved. And the owner will
cheat you if he can. Being Christian, he says he gives his
profits to the basilica, but he lives in the biggest house in
town and owns the most slaves and beats them if they linger at a task." In earlier times, "basilica" had meant a
meeting hall; in Christian terminology, it meant a church.

"Nod!" It was his mother, calling from the courtyard in their house across the street.

"Well then, we shall sleep in our pilentum."

"Ha! And ply your trade, no doubt." Aglow with Stella's light, he had forgotten those dark thunderclouds, the disapproving Christians in the crowd. He did not know the darkest of the clouds, a hooded crone whose close-set eyes peered lightnings from her hood in search of sins to smite. He knew—and well—the priest, a rounded dormouse of a man who preached in the basillica and boasted of his converts from the hard, proud faith of Mithras and the Powers of Light. Conversions were innumerable since Constantine had recognized (though not espoused) the Christian cause. The Emperor's father, Constantius, had stopped the persecutions; the son, the Christians claimed, with their facility for borrowing attributes from other faiths, enjoyed visions from the One True God.

"You had best not park in the city," said Nod.

"Not in the city? But there are other vehicles, and far less clean. Carts, wagons, carriages. . . ." The marketplace was thronged with them, and people, lifting robes to step from stone to stone and miss the mud; the women, twirling parasols like aerial morning glories; the slaves attendant on their mistresses.

"That's just it," he said. "Too crowded." Too many Christians, he thought. Too many womanizers like me.

"Still, a lovely town," she said. A less discerning eye would have encompassed merely streets and mud, paralleled with drains; rectangular divisions—shop and house and meeting hall—named *insulae*; and on the higher, northern hill, a gray basilica, a potters' factory, and platformed temples seeking, like the ladies, to avoid the mud. "It makes me want to weep," she said. "The gentle hills. The lower burnished with its shop and house, like wheat in tidy rows. The upper rich with temples, like a garden sewn by Venus, Rome's imperial mother, but still at heart a sylvan deity in love with flowers. Painted pediments— red and orange and blue—and roofs with terra cotta gods in attitudes of play; inverted crocuses, they seem. Miles away, we thought it really wheat and flowers, this town of yours, as in the Golden Age. Even close at hand it's—"

"It *is* a lovely town," he said. "And nearly as old as Rome. It wasn't used for centuries, you see. Not since the Gauls ransacked the place. Time, the rain, the winds were kind. Thus, it was reoccupied. New houses built, and temples, and—"

"And a basilica," she sighed. "I see a Christian everywhere I look. Their robes resemble winding sheets. Their faces look as if their owners had been wound and buried for at least a month."

"I miss those old Etruscans and their happy ways. Pointed shoes. Hats like little rounded pyramids."

"Tumuli," she said. "I love the ancient words."

"Yes, tumuli. And robes to make a rainbow fade with envy. Especially orange." (A tactful lie in view of Stella's carriage with its orange hood.) "And joy in every face. Why, even death was just a path to better banquetings and sweeter flutes."

Curiously, they did not ask about his yellow hair, among the Roman brown (or saffron dye for ladies of the ancient faith). They looked as if they knew; he almost asked them *what* they knew.

"When there were only Etruscans. . . ." Stella mused. "Etruscan gods of wood and stream and tree. And little Tages found between the furrows of a field. The gray-haired boy whose wisdom helped to build a town."

"Found in a field, you say?"

"Like you."

(How could she know?)

"The Age of Bronze, if not of Gold. Ours is the Age of Tin. Well, Ceres knows it never does to sigh for olden times."

"The Christians sigh for future comings."

"A worse mistake. Today is now. Now is enough." She had reclaimed her smile.

"Sufficient unto the day are the evils thereof." His father sometimes taught him Christian aphorisms, stolen, mostly, from the old philosophers.

"Sufficient unto the day are the joys thereof."

"I like your version better," he confessed. "But then it's *you* I like." He took her hand without embarrassment. He was too young to hide his heart from her.

"I know, my dear," she said, her hand a good luck swallow in his fingers' nest. "I know, my golden Nod. Pomegranate cheeks and wheaten hair. How should I not?"

He fought to hide his tears. (His father often preached of stoicism, valor, pride; his father had no tears.) Was it her loveliness which stirred his heart? Loveliness and *ancientness*. Oh, she was young to see, older than maiden, younger than mother goddess; twenty-five, he would have judged. But aeons seemed to swirl within her eyes, the blue subsiding into amethyst and dimming into gray as shadows fell across the low-roofed town. She might have watched the flight of Saturn and the Golden Age. Watched and grieved; concealed the grief and donned a smile as actors don their masks; learned to live for now and laugh in truth; but not forgotten then, and how a white-haired king had nested singing birds within his beard, and held the Centaur colt, the Satyr kid, the demi-gods of freer, kinder folk. His mother called him "Merry Nod." "Sweet dreams," she liked to say, as if she feared a bitter dream, a memory-curse, might break across his sleep, his waking smile, a shadow on a plot of crocuses. Was Stella memory or curse or both?

"You can park in the fields to the south of the town," he said. "Don't be afraid of wolves. They've fled into Gaul. Not that the citizens would hurt you either. Bodily, that is. But the Christians might offend you with their stares. Sanctimonious, don't you know. Then there are still some pagan folk like me. We stare too, but for a different cause." Roguish Nod, he thought. But who could lie to *her*?

"Sanctimonious stares. In view of all you say, I think we'd better park outside the town. Better for the mules as well as us. They like to browse among the fields. But Nod—about the wolves. Below the town, we saw a— something—wolf, or crouching man, it was hard to say. Hairy and watchful."

"You saw Cedalion, or so he's called. Greek name, I

think. The Worker. He doesn't come to town. They say he's made a tomb into a house and works an ancient mine. They say his helpers are—" No need to frighten her with tales which might be myths. No one had *seen* the six-limbed helpers (so the story ran), the bulbous heads, the legs with hooks instead of feet. They had only seen Cedalion from the fields; the Beast Man so they called him for his hairy chest; and head, a swirl of hair which might be fur. The farmers fled from him and shunned his cave as if it were a passage to the Underworld.

"He didn't exactly frighten me," said Stella. "Whatever he was. It was just that he looked—solitary. An animal without its mate. A man without his woman."

"And what about us?" asked Tutelina, hopeful, not in-sistent. "The mules can browse, but we prefer a more substantial fare than onion grass and stolen grapes."

"I'll bring you bread and cheese from my mother's larder."

"And wine, perhaps?" A grateful blink.

"Of course. Muscatel, the old Etruscan drink. Even Christians may partake of wine, though the wonder's that they haven't switched to milk, since wine can make you feel so—roseate." (Or so he judged by watching revellers return from Isis' rites; the Christians did not revel in their basilica). "But then, Christ turned water into wine, so I suppose it's all right with them. But now I have to go. My mother's calling me to supper." He could not think of any other call which might have taken him from Stella and her friend.

"Later then," smiled Stella. "Tutelina will help me to make you welcome."

"Oh, that's all right, she needn't help. I feel welcome already. She may want to see the town, while you stay in the carriage to tidy up and entertain your first guest. I don't insist on two hostesses. I doubt there's room for three of us at once." He thought: a carriage lit by candle-light and occupied by one with much to teach, and one with much to learn and such a willingness that any teacher must be proud of him.

"Two mistresses are none too many for a harvest festival."

"In a *carriage*?"

"In the fields, of course."

"I must admit I've never seen a harvest festival, what with all this talk of Mithras, Christ, and Isis, who prefer a temple or basilica to open fields. The gods of the field—Ceres and the rest—they've dwindled or died, haven't they?"

"So have Italian harvests. Look at the fields around us. Ripe grapes and wheat and olive trees. Neat, well ordered, pleasing to the eye. But not—"

"Bounteous."

"Exactly."

Like you, he longed to say. "What you have in mind is the old style festival. Leaping over bonfires. Singing incantations. Purifying the fields with sulphur and bean straw?"

"And of course the merrymaking."

"Wine, you mean. Dancing."

"Lots of wine. Dancing such as you never saw. And—"

"And—"

"Why, the most important thing of all. The plants don't flourish from the wine spilled on the ground or from the dancers' feet, bruising the soil like so many blows of a rake. They flourish to the worshipping *induced* by wine and dancing and the other shows of joy."

"Gratitude. Thanksgiving."

"Nod, that's Christian talk. There's more to harvest festivals than you appear to know."

"My parents may be Christian," he replied, "and serve one god, the Desert King. But secretly I pray to several gods, whichever I choose. Goddesses too," he added. "*Particularly* Venus."

"Then you will not be shocked if I tell you that every true festival is climaxed by an orgy."

"Are you very tired from your journey? We might start getting ready now, you know. I had better put on something I can take off in a hurry, hadn't I? Then I can round up some sulphur and bean straws, and it's easy enough to lay a bonfire."

"NOD!"

Stella smiled: "Go to your mother but come to me tonight."

He loved his mother though he could not love her god. She wore a crucifix and strung a lesser cross around his own bare neck, while pagan boys—those at least from ancient families who traced their lineage to the Rome of Romulus or even Aeneas' Troy—wore bullae holding phalluses to honor Mutunus, fertility, and fun. (Secretly he hung a phallus lower than his crucifix; an inexperienced boy like Nod must cultivate virility, and any sexless God was not his god; true, the Christians claimed their Desert King had sired a son, but what he used to plant his seed was said to be invisible and thus, to Nod at least, unenviable.) She often smiled. She often handed him a coin (father not in sight) and urged him to the marketplace: "Your sandal needs a clasp, and buy a salted eel to nibble while you wait." He was a boy who liked to touch the things he loved—a horse, the image of a tutelary god, and most of all the lady who had found him in the fields. The years had bowed her, making white of gray, but still she somehow seemed to shine. She seemed to him a spinning wheel and bread and homespun, and the empty niche which Vesta, lady of the hearth, had shared with the Penates and the Lares of the house in earlier days. If she was Christianity, why, then, he would have joined Christ. But men, it seemed, his father and his friends, contrived to shape the faith, and women followed them.

"Now, my dear"—pretending to be vexed—"I have called you a dozen times. . . . Your father's patience is a trifle thin these days." (Thin? Invisible.) "Come now. He's waiting at the table for his son. He spent the afternoon arranging things. The cellar, don't you know."

How could he know? His father kept the key. Crucifixes . . . images of fish . . . gifts to buy his place in heaven from a god who counted offerings as Croesus counted gold? "Then a visit to the marketplace. He's tired. He wants to eat."

Couches spoke of Rome in earlier times, couches suited pagans bent on lechery; the Lord had used a bench of rough-hewn wood (or so Nod heard at every meal).

Their bench was more than rough; its splinters pierced
the coarse thick wool of toga, tunic, loin cloth, that multiple imprisonment of cloth, designed to hide a body made
for sin. They bowed their heads before a meal more
suited to a sparrow than a boy anticipating harvest festivals and that which climaxed them—cheese, barley
cakes, and gruel—and offered prayers to God. (In pagan
houses, wine was spilled to honor Lar, the spirit of the
house.) Then, a reprimand for children late to meals.

Then, the conversation; no, the monologue. . . .

"Harlots," he said. "Two of them. Right out of Babylon. Constantine has recognized our faith. But when will
he *proclaim*?"

"Harlots?" cried Nod. "I've talked to them. I found
them charming ladies from the south."

"The Devil's servants have been taught to charm. How
else do they allure the folk of Christ?"

"You haven't seen them, my dear," his mother said.
"How can you be so sure that they are what you say?"

"I've heard. They left an invitation in the market place.
Dyed hair and scarlet lips. Etruscan women used to dye
their hair. And what were they?"

"Their kinsmen built this town," Nod said. "This very
house. When Rome was young."

"For wenching. Imbibing. Gluttony. But now the pagan
usurper Licinius is dead, slain at Adrianople, and Constantine is Emperor of Rome, both East and West. And
God, it's said, assured his victory. Mark my words, the
Emperor is just and dutiful, even if slow. The gods shall
surely yield to God, and all of Rome be one basilica." A
Misnan by his birth, a captain seeking fortune on the seas,
Marcus had received more wounds than wealth. To Nod's
dismay, he sometimes beached his ship—no Roman sailed
in winter months, or fall, if seas were rough—and super-
vised his fields of olive tree and wheat and vine.

"It isn't dyed."

"What?"

"The hair. Stella's hair. Tutelina's."

"How do you know, Goldilocks?"

"I looked at the roots."

"A woman's hair is a snare and a temptation. Your mother's head is never bare. Remember Samson. You should not look at tresses, much less roots. The Lord has cursed you for your alien birth; your comeliness will lead you into sin, unless you stand perpetual guard against your lust and never cease to pray. Girls like those pretty locks of yours. I've seen their amorous stares." (Indeed? To Nod, they had seemed merely curious. Adventures frolicked in his thoughts.) "And did you go with them *into their wagon?*"

"They didn't invite me. But I have an invitation to a— uh—festivity."

"You may leave the table. Go to your room at once."

Secreting bread and cheese beneath his robe, he walked a corridor and climbed a wooden ladder to his loft. A single candle lit the couch and chest and niche wherein he kept his household god. Lordon by name, a god of luck in general, as well as fruitful fields and man's fertility, he had his devotees in Rome, although he was a stranger out of Greece. The wheat he clutched within his outstretched hand, the nakedness which Nod concealed with myrtle leaves whenever fathers took a mind to visit wayward sons, bespoke of earlier times, before false modesty had come into the world. He seemed a brother from the Golden Age. He brought good luck to Nod, who would have struck his father to preserve the god of clay.

"Friend," he said. "Shall I attend the festival?"

Images can look inscrutable; you have to know the signs. He winked approval, smiled, Nod thought, his broadest smile as if to say, "Cast off your robes like me. The Earth loves nakedness in all her kin. Do trees conceal their brown and brawny trunks? Do bears engird their loins with a sheepskin or a string of leaves? You, a boy like me becoming man, need not conceal the badge of your virility. Cast off your robes and join the festival."

Nod began his orgiastic plans. To bread and cheese he now must add some wine.

But wine was stored within his father's labyrinth, and Nod must find the key.

Pandora once unlocked a deadly box.

★ Chapter Three ★

It was an ancient ship, it was a weathered ship; it was built for war, not peace, and Dylan could only abide her three-pronged battering ram and two lidless eyes by sniffing her undiminished wonder of wood scents—fir for the hull; pine for the stepped mast and the oars; plane, ash, and acacia for the hull—and pretending himself a freedman in a British forest, instead of a galley-slave aboard a Roman warship awaiting repairs in the port of Ancona; awaiting return to patrol the coasts of Britannia, battle Saxon pirates and uncharted shoals, and strain at his oar until it seemed that he and the wood were one, inseparable in work and pain.

Night hushed the city of potter's wheel and fishwife's complaint, of sailor's chatter and carpenter's hammer and saw; of the multifarious sounds in Italia's largest city on the Adriatic. The masts of a hundred ships, sails furled or lowered and stacked on deck, were a winter-leafless woodland which, if not a shelter, at least did not affright him. The air, it was true, retained the odors of day, the sweat and tar and fish, but such was his weariness that his sensitive nostrils did not take offense. The railings of his ship, the stretched tarpaulin above his head, seemed to gather around him and muffle him into sleep. The eyes on the bow would have closed their lids, he thought, had they lids to close; the raised hurricane deck was free of men; the wicker deck house was dark and empty, the captain visiting a brothel in the town.

A single lantern at the top of the ladder . . . a single guard, drowsing. . . . Otherwise, darkness, peace, and gathering sleep.

"If you please, Sir. My name is Mara."

He opened his eyes, his senses quick and sharp. (He had lived in a sea with sharks and Shelleycoats.)

34

"If you please, I have come to help you escape."

A roving spirit, he thought. A Lamia come to drink his blood. Whirlpools seemed to thump in his brain.

"Have you no tongue?" she snapped. Her stubby wings betokened a Siren child.

"Name o' Dylan," he said, wary. Sirens and sailors had never been friends. "Canna feel my chains." For a year (or a hundred?) he had been shackled, ankles and waist, to the rower's bench, along with the other slaves, forty-nine of them. Now, liberty must be illusion, deceit, snare.

Hesitantly, hating to break the dream, he stared at the dark circles on his wrists, then at the floor. Catching the fitful light of the lamp at the ladder, his chains lay at his feet like crumpled snakes.

The other rowers continued to sleep.

The girl's smile held mischief and childish fun. "I borrowed the key from *him*." A man without manacles, not a slave, slept on a pallet between the bench and the hurricane deck. Whipmaster. Dylan's naked shoulders had often felt his whip. Once he had tried to break his chains. Once he had called the Captain a ruffer because a fellow oarsman had died from thirst and toil. Thanks to Whipmaster, he wore a cloak of scars instead of seal.

"Dinna un'erstand." Captivity had improved his Latin but not erased the lingerings of the earlier tongue.

She blushed; yes, he could see her blush. The smooth, pale cheeks beneath the silver hair turned dark in the faint lantern light.

"Sir, you must hurry. And whisper, please. The guard at the ladder will wake and overhear us." Mara's voice fell in formal syllables; she was speaking Latin, not the tongue of her race. Still, she had the look of a child embarking upon her first adventure.

"What do you want o' me?" he whispered. Since his capture in Caledonia by Walrus and the slavers, everybody had wanted something of him, strength, liberty, youth. . . . (He had not been sold as a stud because he had bitten his would-be purchaser on the flank and stomped her husband's foot.)

"Only to free you. Can you still swim?" Her resolute

actions belied her thin child's voice; she was used to having her way.

"Swim?" He cried. "As soon forget to walk."

"Hush." Soft but peremptory.

He lowered his voice. "Fast as ever, 'spect. Had I my sealskin cloak."

"Here," she said, presenting him with a large, furry rag.

"What's that?"

"The sail is lined with fur."

"I know. Hyaena and seal and—"

"I was careful to choose the seal. The hyaena parts were all mangy. Besides, hyaenas don't swim. They just eat."

"Got some shears?" Nothing would surprise him about the girl.

"Teeth are just as good." She opened her mouth to display a perfect, pearly row which even a Roane must admire. He remembered a Siren's favorite dish, and a certain tale, told to him by his mates, of how Ulysses had lost a part of his crew to Siren songs.

She arranged the rag across his shoulders and back, tenderly, fussily, as if she were mimicking gestures observed in a human woman, as if his scars, though fading, were open and raw.

"Come." She clambered onto the railing, between the shields which protected the rowers from enemy missiles, and entered the water with no more sound than the flick of a minnow's tail. He followed her into their mutual, natural element.

"How far can you swim?" she asked as they glided and twisted among the forest of ships.

"A whole day wi'out stoppin'."

"Splendid," she said. "I wasn't sure about Roanes. You won't have to swim that far. There's a sea-cave just to the north. . . ."

"You see," she said, "even a Siren likes a nest. We don't spend all of our time in the sea, unless we must. For visiting, the land is better." (And dining? On many a beach, he had seen the scattered bones from a Siren's feast. The race had a genius for sensing ships in trouble and rushing to help them sink by gnawing holes in the hull and helping to drown the men.)

"Got any parents, kid?" he blurted.

"Devoured by Cyclopes," she said. "A few of the monsters are still about, you know, in the Misty Isles, and mean as—as. . . ." Usually decisive, she faltered into silence. There was nothing as mean as a Cyclops (except, it was said, a Siren rejected in love or denied a meal).

"And you look after yourself, do you?" he asked, dreading to hear about a flock in the environs. (Yes, flock was the word, not school; for the Sirens yearned to the time when their wings had carried them over the land and sea; now, they must carry their useless wings beneath the sea, eternally exiled by the Great Mother because of their gruesome ways.)

"Well enough. Most of my people avoid the coasts of Italia. The Christians call us demons, you see."

(*Got a point for once, them Christians.*)

He saw the litter of bones on this particular bank and wondered who or what had provided them. The roof of the cave was luminescent, a coruscation of many-colored stones, and showed the interior with fearful clarity, not only the bones but broken shells, ships' spars, rusting anchors, and other watery relics. Thank Neptune, most of the bones appeared to have come from fish. The builder in him, the boy who had wanted a tidy house and built an eminently habitable coracle, wrinkled his nose, tried to ignore the refuse, but admired the couch which Mara had wrought from seemlier materials; sea-wrack neatened into a rectangle and bordered with murex and conch; coverlit spun from the filaments of a Pegasus-fish (angel-fish to a Christian): casque of driftwood for holding gemstones— lapis lazuli, coral, pink and white, aquamarine, tourmaline, amber. A lobster's cave, he thought. Objects gathered for no other reason than quantity and variety. But then he discerned a pattern reflecting the taste, indeed the character, of the collector. The bones and the broken shells: sinister, destructive. The gemstones and the care-

fully ordered couch: domestic, comfortable, even beautiful. Mara mirrored the sea, in herself and her cave.

Dylan began to like her and feel at home. Until she
spoke:

"I do miss the feasts we had here when I was young.
Once a merchant ship went down, and we held a festival
for a solid week. Oh, they were wicked people, the pas-
sengers, all of them. Fat, pampered women in garish jewels, with wigs or dyed hair. A crew who spoke the foulest
language you can imagine. A captain who had an eye for
the women instead of his ship. Well, we wingéd ladies got
him in the end."

"Hungry now, kid?"

"If you call me kid again," she snapped. "I just might
work up an appetite."

"Dinna mean offense."

"No?"

"Nay. Lost my maers on the galley. Should've said
thank you."

"Think nothing of it," she said.

"Think a lot of it. Feel like a ruffer."

"You mean ruffian."

"Mean what I said. Ruffer. Same as blackguard, only
not as bad."

"Your speech is funny. It's as if you had a cockleburr
under your tongue, and the words—sometimes I don't
know what they mean, but I still like them. Here," she
said, drawing him to a seat on an empty cask. "Rest.
Then I expect you must go."

"Go?" He had spent a year in goings. He had gone
from the galley; now he wanted to stay. "Where?"

"Wherever you choose."

"Britannia," he said. "Forests all over the place—rivers
too. Never got ashore, though."

"Then you must build or steal a boat to get you there."

"Steal?" He had never stolen the smallest object, not
even a morsel of food from a fellow slave.

"Build it then. But your ears have funny holes. For
earrings?"

"Mark of a slave," he barked.

"And the marks on your back," she said with a rue which he had not thought to find in her race. "You can hide the shoulders but not the ears. In the East, the men wear earrings, but here they would brand you for a runaway. Until you build your ship, you must keep out of sight."

"Where?"

"There're underground rivers that lead to the north. And forests. And resin. Whatever you need."

"Like to—like to come wi' me?" he stammered. She was the first girl he had ever met. Oh, he had seen a multitude from his bench in the ship. Harlots with puckering lips like those of a fish on the beach; slaves who never dared to lift their eyes. Met only her. Breastless, almost hipless, she might have been a boy with long hair and a sweet, piping voice. A—what was the word?—catamite. No. It was more than breasts and swelling hips which constituted a girl. What was the nature of "more" he could not say. Was it—enigma? The sea was a god to men on the shore. To sailors, it was a goddess, who went by many names, but many names could not conceal the One. Mara was a child of the One. He did not want to lose her, his friend from the sea. He wanted to teach her to fish (but of course she already knew), to clean a coracle (that she must learn, for Sirens were slovenly), to sing to him in sweet but not ensorceling notes. He wanted to learn from her of sunken ships and hidden caves and how to predict a squall or hide from a tidal wave. He wanted to ask if her wings encumbered her in the sea, and where she had found the amber fibulae in her hair, and why she had legs instead of a tail, but even without a cloak could outswim a Roane.

"Canna go wi' me?"

"No," she sighed, child in truth, tears pearling her eyes. "I have to stay in the sea. Water is life to me. I can walk on the land—a little while—but then I wilt and die."

"Could go wi *you*."

She gave him a sudden hug, then withdrew, embarrassed, but not before he had hugged her in return.

She shook her head. "I can swim from here to Britannia without touching land. You need the land as much as the sea."

"Yea," he admitted, thinking of Caledonian coracles, safety from sharks and Merrows (if not from slavers). "Well then—"

"Well then." The lostness in her voice did not match her words.

"Why maun you save me, Mara?"

"Because I must."

"Ain't no answer."

She turned away from him; her hair was caught by a pierced scallop shell in a braid behind her back. "You are a thief."

"Thief?" he protested. "What have I stole?"

"My wings."

"Still on your back!" Then he understood the truth of her charge. The wings of a Siren held her emotions, like the heart in a Roane or a man. ("My wings ache for you," a Siren would say.)

"Dinna mean to."

"I spied you at your oar. Followed your ship from the Pillars of Hercules. Saw that awful Whipmaster lash you with his whip. I thought you would surely bleed to death. You never uttered a cry. You were so strong. So— fetching. You stole my wings."

"Canna give 'em back. Don't know how."

"I'll grow up," she said, "and steal *your* wings."

"Haven't any."

"Heart, I mean."

"Yea?"

"Will you save it for me?"

"Take part o' it now." His own offer amazed him; he hardly knew the girl, and cannibalism was not to his taste. He had not learned that love and time do not walk hand in hand.

"I want *all* of it." Thus she betrayed her race. No men to protect them, propagating like spiders by males whom they captured and sometimes ate, betrayed so they thought even by their goddess, they had learned to fend for themselves, and fended so well that what they wanted they usually found. Thanks to Bonus Eventus, she wanted a sweetheart instead of a meal. For the moment, at least.

Slowly, he shook his head. "Canna promise." He could not foresee the future, in spite of his sealskin cloak. He could only foresee—change. A greater freedom than from his bench in the galley? A new and harsher bondage? An irresistible thief? "Canna promise."

"No matter. Wait till you see me grown. Remember what my ancestors did to Ulysses."

"Almost et him."

"I didn't mean *that*. I meant lured. With their silvery tresses, all asparkle like foam with sunlight. And their witching songs. See, I can already sing:

'Who will come to stay;
Going, say good-bye?
Love has gone away,
Love, the dragonfly.' "

She had entered the nest of his heart; stolen, fledgling wren, into the corner reserved for little sisters. But the center, the holy of holies, remained inviolate, awaiting the one belovéd.

And so he began his journey up the river.

★ Chapter Four ★

Companioned only by a fitful lamp and holding to the key extracted from his father's money pouch, he had, it seemed, unlocked the realm of Dis, the god of death. (Stella, he thought. Only for you.) The long and ragged flight of stairs wrenched from the earth had not bespoken casks of wine awaiting at the foot; still, his father had emerged from his mysterious descents with wine and only wine; a pigskin in the days before he had assumed the Christian faith; a simple flagon, wrought of fired clay, since Christianity had further darkened and subdued his ways.

If not a wealth of wine, why, then, some Christian artifacts, Nod thought, to hush the voice which whispered, "Watch your step, my boy." A crucifix, that gruesome relic of a godling's death. A shrine perhaps where Christian men commune with God; a god too lordly for a woman and a boy; the stern and bearded giant adored as Yahweh or the Desert King, jealous and cruel, and doom to cities whose inhabitants preferred the Lady with her many faces and her single love. Sodom and Gomorrah ... Jericho. ...

But in the fickle sputter of his lamp, he saw a space which might have been a tomb with several openings like dusky mouths into a deeper earth; a tomb such as the sad Etruscans dug in after days, when Rome was threatening their dwindled power and they foresaw defeat in life and could not contemplate a happy afterlife. No longer hunts and games and banquetings; nor men on horseback, youths and maidens dancing to a double flute; divers, nude and sun-embraced, arising from a sea where dolphins sported like a circus troop.

Instead, funerary urns like bloated skulls; muraled walls depicting perils on the highway to the throne of

Pluto—Dis, the Romans said—and his grave, stolen
queen, Proserpine; Cerberus, the triple-headed dog;
Charon, that gray ferryman, and demons by the multitude
... ovine, equine, lupine ... tails like whips for insubor-
dinate slaves ... horns to please a Minotaur, that monster
born of an unholy liaison between a queen and bull . . .
hooves, but not for dancing under harvest moons.

Demons ... nightmares from the pagan underworld,
enemies of men who worshipped spirits of the upper air.
Such beings had escaped before the coming of the Christ,
or so his father said, and hidden in the North, or stolen
ships and sailed to Caledonia through the Nether Seas.

In such a place he might discover skulls. He sniffed for
mushrooms, lichens, roots, especially wine, the distillation
of the bounteous grape—any growing thing—but death,
not growth, was emperor in this tomb. He turned to
mount the stairs. So much for Stella's wine. Perhaps a
flagon smuggled from the dining room. . . .

Then he saw the hoofprints in the dust and caught a
lingering smell: decomposing flesh and fetid breath.

"Jove," he swore. "If I were Roustabout instead of
Goldilocks!" He flexed his muscles, felt them firm but
small, and wished himself into a Hercules. He sensed the
imminent return of—something—man or beast—and father to no child except a ghoul. Well, he did not need to
wait and meet the owner of the room. The stairs became
his friends, like helpful rabbits standing on each other's
backs.

Except. . . .

Something slouched between him and the stairs, a living gate.

A demon in the flesh, more rat than man, though walk-
ing on two legs. His face was smooth and white, his fur so
short that it could pass for night-bleached skin; the alto-
gether furless tail athwart the air as if it were a hawser
from a rotting ship. Red lidless eyes; the only hair, black
forks upon the brows; the open mouth, an aperture re-
vealing scarlet tongue and close-packed, ragged teeth. A
monstrous rat in whose contorted face he seemed to read
remembrances of being small and chased and trapped,

loathsome to man, furtive for want of size; now, suddenly enlarged, intent upon revenge.

He rid his mind of such a fantasy. Here was no rat. Here was a demon born demoniac. The horns . . . the hooves . . . the forkéd tail . . . the living likeness of a demon on the wall. Here was a murderer of souls, and bodies holding souls; never small; pursuer, not pursued.

"Sir," he said, atremble underneath his weight of robes. He would not beg, not even for his life. He would explain, request, and if denied, outwit. Demons, he had heard, were lions in strength but geese in intellect. "I only came to find some wine." (If he could smell a single, starveling root. . . .)

Hydra-quick, the slouch became a pounce; the demon seized Nod's shoulder in a bruising grip. Nod almost dropped his lamp. He clung tenaciously to that poor source of light.

Could old Etruscan demons understand the Latin tongue?

"I—only—came," he said as one might start a sentence to a child.

"This my domicile. You are a thief or spy. The scent of you is bitter like the grass." The careful Latin would have pleased a Cicero. The tone was deep but strangely feminine. He scrutinized the beast and saw vestigial breasts and swelling hips. He saw the lack of what he owned but had not exercised. True, she did not match the naked women on the walls of older tombs—dancers, flutists, divers—his only glimpse of woman's nudity. (His mother hid her body as a leper hides her ravaged flesh.) Their mysteries disclosed, they did not lose their lure. Borrowing from the poets, he thought of them as gardens: melons, berries, grapes; secret crevices of mint and thyme; a place to satisfy a hunger more imperative than that for food; and best of all, a harvest-home of flaxen hair, or riches tempting man to couch and smooth and toss and wreathe his face in their sweet undulance.

This garden was a rat.

"I see that now. I didn't at first, though. Can't you consider me a sort of unexpected but not unwelcome guest?

My mother always says that *everyone* is welcome at her door."

"Guests bring gifts. What have you brought me, Goldi-locks?"

"If you will let me past, I'll fetch you some cheese."

"Cheese is for rats."

He bit his tongue before he said, "Why then, you should feed very well." Instead. "Oh no, not my mother's cheese. You ought to see the cow who gives her milk."

"Cheese, milk, cows, what do you take me for, a milk maid? Better a pretty boy than twenty rounds of cheese."

By Juno's holy breast, she meant to take her pleasure with him in the tomb! Etruscan matrons, he recalled, had fancied boys.

"I'm still a virgin," he announced, for once not loathe to advertise the fact.

"It was digestion I had in mind, not seduction."

A more experienced boy, he had no doubt, an em-peror's minion or a lady's darling, could flaunt his assets and divert her thoughts from food. But how to tempt a demon from a feast? Seduce or be seduced and in the process make a hurried flight? His furtive reading in the *Satyricon* had left him uninformed for such a confronta-tion in the flesh. Being a virgin boy with Christian parents—well, he felt like Noah swallowed by the whale. He thought of David and his many wives (and concu-bines). He thought of Samson wenching in Philistia (be-fore he lost his locks). But wives and concubines were strange to him. Stella, he had thought, would demonstrate erotic niceties.

Nod, the time has come to improvise. Divert the demon or become her meal. Those pretty boys, they entertained the matrons with a wealth of tricks.

It was a way he had of talking in his head. Unfriended in a town where other boys had dusky hair and knew their origins, he often sought his private dreams for friends.

Gymnasts, flutists, acrobats, he thought, tricksters all of them. Chariot races. Dancing horses drawn on platforms

with tremendous wheels. He had watched travelling circuses and longed to be an acrobat.

"Would you reconsider," he asked, "about the meal, I
mean. That is, if I were to *put forth*?" The verb, being
vague, allowed a certain latitude.

She seemed to laugh. At least she made a rumbling
sound and he could see the sharpness of her teeth. "Dear
boy, I prefer experience to youth, and dinner to dal-
liance."

"I can do acrobatics," he said. "Turn cartwheels.
Somersaults. I watched the gymnasts in a circus once and
learned their tricks."

"Raw or roasted," she mused. "Have you a preference,
Goldilocks?"

"I'm good at other things. Versatile, don't you know."

"Raw, I should think. Spitting, seasoning, turning—too
much wasted time. Domestic skills have never been my
forte."

"You're quite determined to, er, make a meal of me?"

"Such a wait," she sighed, "since I devoured a full-
fledged boy. The Etruscans used to bring me babies—
fondlings—payment, don't you see, to keep their tombs
for them. Mere appetizers, though. No juicy, strapping
boys unless I foraged on my own. Not that you're strapping. Juicy though, and easier to chew."

"Madame, I *do* have muscles," he protested. "It's just
that they're underneath the skin. Greek, you see, and not
the rangy Roman kind. But tough. Extremely tough."

"Well, I shall feast, and not set foot into the hateful
sun!"

She caught him in an angular embrace. He felt the hot
stench of her breath upon his face and wished a toothrag
for her ancient mouth, and myrrh and frankincense to
slosh upon her mimicry of breasts, and carmine to incar-
nadine her cheeks; and loss of appetite.

"I sing, you know," he gasped.

"What?"

"Christian hymns, for one."

"Ha!" She laughed and flung him free of her. "Sing for

my supper, will you? Ah, Goldilocks, you've given me a laugh."

"You see," he said, "I *can* entertain. I made you laugh. When I have my own circus, I shall tell jokes and—"

"Very well then. Sing if you must, and dance, and tell some raunchy jokes. First, however, robes will have to go." He stood before her in his loin cloth, an oddment of discarded linen from his mother's loom. She looked at him with unconcealed disgust.

"Ugh. You're sunburned. Myself, I like a whiter skin. Well, I can always peel you."

"I till my father's fields. You can't till in a toga."

"Never mind, on with the song and the jokes."

Stupid rat, he thought. Where do you think a boy with Christian parents learns to dance? He called to mind the old Etruscan paintings he had seen of youth or maiden dancing to the sound of nameless instruments. He fancied flutes, sweet and melancholy—imprisoned throats of nightingales, the poets said of them. He fell into the music of his mind, arms afloat upon the air, yellow hair aswirl about his head (a nimbus, *not* a halo for a saint).

"I said dance, not weave about as if you were going to faint. Let's not risk the meat."

He fancied drumbeats, stomped his foot as if he meant to march to war.

"That's more like it. Now let yourself go. Snap those fingers. Toss those pretty curls."

"Jesus, saviour of my soul,
I, a lambkin in your fold. . . ."

A foolish choice of a metaphor.

"More like a full-grown lamb," she smirked.

"Jesus, hearken to my prayer,
Guard me from the scroungy bear,
May the thievish gutter rat
Rob, instead of me, the cat. . . ."

Unpalatable animals, to say the least, calculated to reduce appetite, and with an intimation, doubtless too dense for her slow brain, that she was both scroungy and thievish.

"I didn't ask for a prayer, and I didn't ask to be compared to a bear and a rat. I asked for *something raunchy.*"

If he lacked experience, at least he compensated in imagination. He had enjoyed an ample share of racy thoughts; furtive kisses snatched from Christian girls; pats exchanged between the pews in the basilica. He improvised a dirty song and sang it in a voice which, unmelodious, at least was suitable to such a theme.

The Satyr and the Seraph

When Earth had lost her artless infancy,
A satyr met a seraph in a grove.
The satyr, tempted by her wings of mauve,
The seraph, unseraphic for an hour,
Exchanged the token of a passion flower
And sinned, begetting my ancestral tree.
Today, the frugal forest of myself
Is seraph-kept from satyr, faun, and elf,
But through the trees a satyr still may peep.
Ah, seraph, seraph, will you *never* sleep
And let him frolic in the woods of me?

"I hope you're a better dinner than a poet. I never heard such a Gorgon's brew of names and styles. Have you forgotten your hexameters? And what is a Greek satyr doing in a Latin poem? And what, by the holy rod of Dis, is an elf?"

"A poem should not be explained," he said. "A poem *is.* Never question a poet about his meaning. He listens to his Muse and—"

"Your Muse must have been drunk on pomegranate wine. Still, you've given me a laugh. But now it's time to dine." Her white arms wriggled toward him in a caricature of love.

He had exhausted dances, games, and songs. Perhaps a compliment would win him time for further stratagems.

"Do you know," he said, wanting to bite his tongue, "I

have never seen a naked breast. Only painted ones on
walls. I must confess that yours are *quite* unusual."

"They are, aren't they?" A show of teeth. "Observe
their whiteness and their delicacy. (Invisibility.) "Love
apples, you might say." (Acorns from a stunted oak.)

"And those black eyebrows, topped with scarlet
horns—"

"You'll not find such above the ground," she beamed.
"Come now, Goldilocks." (Her grip becoming bronze.)
"You understand, I harbor no ill will. A quick decapita-
tion, little pain. If you had angered me, I would have
done you toe by tender toe. Now. Remove your loin
cloth. Cross and image too. The way you Romans like to
gird yourselves, I'd rather pluck a goose then peel a boy."

"Very well then." Reluctantly, he parted with his light,
his lamp of olive oil, and placed it carefully beside his
feet. Reluctantly he folded his discarded, crimson-bor-
dered toga and unclasped the pin which held his loin
cloth. He poised, indeed he lingered on the pin, with mar-
tial thoughts.

"Modest, are we, Goldilocks? Snap to it. I had a friend
who choked on a loin cloth."

"First the sandals," he said, kneeling by the lamp as if
to loose his straps.

Rising, he flung hot oil into the demon's face.

She shrieked, half rage, half pain, and raised her hands
to guard her wounded eyes.

Those dusky mouths, those other exits from the room
than stairs—better an earthen mouth than one of gaping
flesh. Better stones than teeth.

He chose the nearest mouth, and he was gone, mercurial, down its throat. . . .

Lightless, the tunnel stretched ahead of him, the light
behind him dwindling into dark. He scraped his head on
roots, he lunged and ducked and ran a crouching race, he
lurched from wall to wall, collecting dirt and bruises as he
went. Then, outstretching hands to keep himself from further earthen blows, he struck a steady pace . . . down . . .
sharply down . . . into the labyrinths of Dis, the Lord of

G. Barr

Death, or Vulcan, whose volcanic wrath had buried Herculaneum and Pompeii. Hell, a Christian might have said.

He paused to catch his breath. The smell of death enveloped him like some malarial mist from those forsaken towns which, skeletal, disfaced the coast of the Tyrrhenian Sea. Earthscents he loved, but not of bones and worms and winding sheets. . . . Was he beneath a human necropolis? The Misnans, now and in the late Etruscan times, interred their dead within the city walls. Yet he had run at least a mile. What ancient tombs, what alien fields, could lie above his head?

He could not hear the footsteps of the demon chasing him. Her height would make pursuit a stumbling, not a race. But could he find the sun without returning through her lair? Return he must. His mother must be warned about the demon underneath her house. His father. . . .?

It came to him at last. The guarded key. His father's trips into his cellar where he kept his "wine." The nickname Goldilocks. Why, he communed with demons after he had prayed in his basilica! Perhaps he brought her food. Perhaps he liked those pallid, wizened breasts and shared the floor with her! Such, his Christianity.

"Mithras and Isis," Nod began to pray. "And Lordon too, little among the least, though much to me. Spare my mother from the demon's appetite." It was, however, not a time for prayer.

He lacked the breath. His legs were numb. He did not know how they could hold his weight. He could not slow for, slowing, he would stop and, stopping, wait to die, a demon's feast.

The tunnel rose invisibly beneath his aching feet. A light, a promise, then a certainty—a room—and waiting arms.

He felt the hair. Not hers, but whose? He fell into those hairy, unknown arms.

★ Chapter Five ★

"Just who the Not-World are you?" barked Dylan.

The lad looked innocuous; semi-conscious, in fact; Dylan's immediate instinct was to make a guest of him. But he had come from Mana's labyrinth. Perhaps he was the innocent he seemed; perhaps himself a demon, slaver, who could say? A year in chains had taught an ill-used Roane to mistrust everybody except for Siren girls.

"Sir," said the lad, faint of voice but ready to fight. "Are you going to kill me?"

"Canna say yet. Demon, are you?"

"A fondling. Roman by adoption. Chased by a demoness—old, hungry, and hideous."

"Genita Mana, the old sea-cow. 'Truscans found her when they come from Lydia. Fed her babies so's she wouldn't eat their dads."

His mongrel dialect, part Latin, Celtic, sailor's slang, would drive a pedagogue to slash his wrists. His untrimmed beard, the tattered sealskin round his shoulders, the impersonation of a loin cloth: *Lad'll take me for a criminal*, he thought. *Well, 'spect I am.*

"How'd a bairn like you get away from her?"

"Bare one, did you say? The old rat stole my clothes."

"*Bairn.* Youngster."

"Out-talked her. Then I threw my lamp in her face." He sniffed the air. "Your room smells of roots and grass. And isn't there sailor's tar?"

"Buildin' a boat," said Dylan, dropping his ferocity but still unwilling to reveal his plans. "Well, old Mana never was much good at talk."

"Who did you say you are, Sir?"

"Dylan. 'Son o' the Waves.' "

"I'm Nod."

"Nod, eh? Don't know what it means. Sounds good, though."

"*Dylan*," Nod mused. "Cedalion you mean!"

"Country folk misname me. Ought to be D-Y-L-A-N."

"But I always thought—"

"Dylan was a beast? Hairy and wild? Just like you, 'cept for my gills and cloak. Ain't even got a tail."

"*Everybody* has a tail. What do you sit on?"

"Fishy kind, I mean."

"I never thought you were a beast."

"Wouldn't blame you if you thought me a' old wolf. Can't keep clean underground. Hair like dirt."

"Not dirt," Nod protested. "Onyx."

"Fancy talk don't help. Dirt." (*Talks like a poet. More Celt than Roman.*) "Fancy a mite o' brew?"

"Wine?"

"Beer. Made it myself out o' hops."

"I never drank any beer."

"Time to try, bein' chased and all, and almost et. Here." He handed Nod a calyx carefully wrought of clay into a Siren's shape. Nod dispatched the beer in one swift gulp.

"More, if you please."

"How old are you, kid?"

"Old enough for a second cup of beer."

"*Mug.* Don't look it. Old enough, I mean."

"I'm *fifteen*."

"Got a year on you. But in the fleet, sixteen goin' on seventeen's downright middle-aged. Man o' the world, I am. Know everythin', and not scroll-learnin' neither. Sailed here from Britannia. Been to Corinth. Eire. Alexandri. You name it, Dylan's been there."

"You're a sailor then?"

"Nay."

"Explorer?"

"Galley slave."

He would have liked to hide his calloused hands, the bulging biceps underneath the cloak, the ankle-marks from brazen chains. He waited for a look of contempt, at least disdain: the usual response to galley slaves.

Nod began to cry.

Small wonder he's ballin', poor mite. Chased by a demon. Saved by a' ugly Roane.

"That's all right, kid. Safe from Mana in Dylan's house."

"I'm—I'm," stammered the boy, "cry—crying for you. A slave. A *galley* slave. You must have been w-whipped, and—all kinds of things."

"Cryin' for *me*?" No one had ever cried for him, except a Siren girl. Roman men withheld their tears and boasted of their pride and manliness. But Nod did not seem Roman with his yellow hair. Tears became him.

He pressed, then dropped, Nod's hand. Familiarity might scare the boy.

"Oh, no," said Nod. "I'm not afraid of you, even if you do bark at times."

"Bark, do I? Like this?" He gave a walrus snort.

Nod pressed his hand and laughed. Smudged from the catacombs, he somehow smelled of bread and grass and cleanliness, and touch from him was eloquence. (In that sweet land of Dylan's birth, had touch not been more eloquent than words? Ah, memory was a cheat. . . .)

Dylan had found a friend. Most friends, he knew, must first be earned and cultivated through the years. Nod? A simple gift. The Celt in him cried, "Celebrate!"

"Like to dance?" he asked (he did not know where he had learned the steps), and jerked the boy into a leap, a dip, a duck, a somersault. Color, picture, furniture enclosed, embraced them like a protean animal. True, the room remained a tomb, but not funereal. The first Etruscans had constructed tombs like houses, habitats of cheer for souls awaiting guides into the Underworld. The walls appeared to leap with life; diners sprawled on couches, women with their men; a spotted cat; a lion with Sphinx's wings. A pride of forest folk from Saturn's Golden Age, all hoof and tail and horn and quaint appendages without a name.

"It's like coming home!" cried Nod. "I'll take you with me to a festival."

"Whose?" Suspicion like a giant squid.

"Stella's."

"The golden woman?"

"Yes. You watched her, she said, as she neared the town."

"The *goddess*."

"Who can say?"

Sadly he shook his head. "Dylan ain't gold."

"Ain't?"

"Sailor's lingo. Dylan's *not* gold."

"I've already told you—"

"Does fire like earth?"

"Stella will like you at once. That is, if you don't bark at her. Possibly, though, if you're going to her festival, you ought to—well, have you ever shaved before?"

"Not since Caledonia. (In truth, he had never shaved. In Caledonia, he had been too young. In the galleys, who had time?)

"I'll bring you a razor." He sounded as if he had shaved for years, or visited barbers in the market place. His cheeks, however, could not even boast of down.

"Don't want to look smooth. Might get caught. Scare people this way."

"But you had a beard in the galley, didn't you? If anybody's following you, he'll be looking for beards. Shaved, you'll be a different man. And Stella likes smooth cheeks."

"Know that for a fact?"

"She never said as much. But it's a harvest festival, and people kiss and all that sort of thing, and who wants to kiss a beard? Or for that matter, *be* kissed by a beard."

"Better shave then." His knowledge of festivals was limited to the talk aboard his ship; the manner in which they included kisses eluded him. Still, he wanted to learn. "See that citron chest under the crossed spears. 'Truscans packed it for their voyage to the Underworld. Tunics, sandals, razors. But what'll I wear?" The robes in the chest were fashioned for smaller men. His sealskin cloak, that which Mara had bitten from the sail, did not appear to suit a festival.

"A loin cloth is fine," Nod said. "Unless you have something, well, more festive."

"How 'bout you?" grinned Dylan, pointing to that pathetic oddment which Mana had not contrived to steal.

"I *had* a tunic and toga. Never mind. Festivals are for shedding clothes."

"Before a *lady*?" The prospect of showing his naked shoulders to Stella appalled him.

"Stella isn't a lady. She's—well, *beyond*. And yes, you'll have to shed. That's the best part, she says. The part the fields enjoy. The orgy."

"Orgy," sighed Dylan, a blush beneath his beard. "Orgify. Means to kiss and hug and pinch and—"

"Don't stop now."

"More." ("More" meant "best.")

"You know all about it then!"

"Oh, yes. Used to orgify back home. 'Mongst the oaks. Wi' Druid priestesses."

"I never learned how myself."

(*Honest kid. Makes me ashamed. Still, I'm older. Got to keep up my sealskin.*)

"I expect it's like learning how to row a boat or build a fire, isn't it?"

"Bit o' both. Harder, though."

"But Dylan, are you sure you haven't forgotten anything? You can't fool Stella, you know. If you have, you'd better admit it and get her advice and instruction. How many orgies have you attended?"

Dylan looked at the wall. A bare-breasted diner seemed to stare reproaches at him. "One," he confessed. "Almost. Captain's wife come to me in the night. 'Captain's ashore wi' a wench,' she said. 'Slaves asleep. Always did fancy me a lad like you.' Couldn't do nothin'! Hard, wi' all them chains. Called me a bloody virgin, she did. Never come back."

"That wasn't an orgy, that was a—what's the Christian word?—mere fornication. Almost. Or adultery? I forget the distinction. As sins go, it's only middling, unless you're a woman. Then you get stoned, I think. At least among the Christians. Of course I don't agree."

(*Kid gets nicer wi' every word.*)

"At least you have a start. I expect you must simply

decide what you did wrong the first time and add a few
embellishments with each new woman."

"Didn't do *nothin'* wrong. Right neither. No chance.
Better teach me, Nod. Must've read about it."

"I can't teach you a thing," admitted Nod. "I've read,
but I didn't understand the subtleties. But Stella will teach
us both."

"Think a lot o' Stella, do you?"

"Yes, I guess I do. It seems too soon, doesn't it?"

"Soon can be forever. Fancy her myself and we ain't
even met."

"Oh, I'm not surprised. She's likable all right."

Dylan felt a fibula prick of jealousy. Stella would surely
prefer the golden Nod to the dusky Dylan (even if
shaved). For Nod was smooth, where he, Dylan, was
rough—in body, speech, and manner. Smooth in the no-
blest sense. Bonus Eventus in the flesh, not slick like
Stoat and scattering compliments for bait.

"Also, she has a friend. Tutelina. Isn't that a pretty
name? Blonde as a tassel of corn, and *very* accomodating.
It might be you would prefer her even to Stella. After all,
you only have to be refreshed. I have to be taught from
scratch."

Dylan grinned. "Refreshed, eh? Sounds like drinkin'
beer wi'out passin' out. Just the glow and the merry talk.
Not even a achin' head." He was remembering the first
Roman vessel, the kindly crew. "High time, ain't it?"

"Isn't, Dylan. When in Rome—"

"Isn't what?"

" 'Ain't' ain't—isn't—grammatical."

Dylan slapped him mightily on the back and shoved
him onto the floor. "Sorry, lad. But time to get movin'."
Then, trumpet-loud: "Angus, bring Dylan a razor. And a
fresh loin cloth. Red. Right color for an orgy, eh, Nod?"

"Perfect."

To Angus: "Find one for my guest!"

"I didn't know you had a servant, Dylan."

"Don't. Friend. Caught by the slavers in Caledonia.
Sold to a travelin' circus. Broke out and sniffed his way
here to me. Don't ask me how."

Six-legged, big as a hunting dog from Macedonia, the Telchin stood in the door to appraise the uninvited guest.

"Dylan, can't you throw him a fish or something? He looks—anticipatory."

"Wheat and berries. That's what he favors."

Angus entered the room and bent, as docilely as a seal, beneath his master's hand.

"I wouldn't have guessed. He has a carnivorous glint to his eyes. I expect he has friends?"

"Used to. All gone though."

"Is he going to the festival with us?"

"Nay. Keeps too sharp an eye on me. What's the word?"

"Prudish?"

"That's it. 'Fraid I'll misbehave. Stella don't like prudes, does she?"

"Stella likes—let's go and see."

Invitations can lead to new friends—or old enemies.

★ Chapter Six ★

Dylan fingered his cheeks, red no doubt, from the dull, antique razor which had shaved the face of an Etruscan gentleman when Rome was a scrappy homunculus instead of a world-bestriding Atlas; and sighed to see the murdered beard reproach him from the floor.

In turn, Nod examined him and admired what he saw: the older brother of his dreams. Dylan's curious speech, his preternatural strength, his service in the galleys: They joined with gentleness to endear the man to him (for Dylan did not seem a boy to sheltered Nod).

He also loved him for his loneliness.

"Naked," sighed Dylan. "Used to the beard. Sort o' a sealskin."

"It makes you look like a bear, not a seal," said Nod, smiling approval at his denuded victim.

"What's wrong wi' bears? Like 'em."

"So do I, but people were afraid of you."

"Meant 'em to be. Kept 'em at a distance. Disguise, don't you see. Didn't want to be caught."

"That man who caught you in Caledonia—what was his name?"

"Never knew. Called him Walrus. Suited."

"He's probably back in the Misty Isles by now."

"Hard to tell. Fat but a sneak. Looked like a walrus. Happened on you like a shark."

"Stella will like you better without your beard."

He turned to Nod with a slow, growing smile. "Will she? Worth it then. Not much to look at, though."

"No?" He brandished a looking glass, retrieved from the burial chest along with the razor, in front of Dylan's face. Dylan closed his eyes.

"Tryin' to witch me, laddie?"

"This is called a mirror."

"Know what it's called. Don't like it. It's eldritch. One o' me's enough."

"Take a look at the second Dylan."

"Don't look like you."

"Better."

"Canna."

"Can."

"Gills and webs look sickly out o' water."

"Different, that's all. Besides, you won't always be out of water."

"Dis, what a stubborn kid. Fooled me at first wi' your easy ways. Hard as a lobster's claw, though, when you make up your mind."

Nod presented the mirror to Dylan. "Well, then, if I'm hard, do what I say. Take a second look at yourself."

Dylan blinked and peered into the mirror's ominous face: handle shaped like a stem; oval a flattened lotus of tarnished bronze.

"Keep on looking."

"It's me before the galley and yet it ain't. Same old eyes, same old teeth, but. . . ."

"It's been—how long?"

"A year or thereabouts. Lose track in the galleys."

"You're older, that's all."

"Old man, Nod?"

"A young man but no longer a boy."

"Good or bad?"

"Good," said Nod. "But there's more to do. I've found a pair of shears."

"Ain't a sheep."

"What do you know about shearing sheep?"

"Saw it from my bench." Roman galleys always hugged the coast unless there were shoals to avoid or islands to reach. "Sheep dies after a shearin', don't it?"

"It grows a new coat. Sit still." He shoved Dylan onto the couch and circled him like a Gallic executioner, who examines his victim to determine the angle for wielding his ax, and straightaway started to cut. Ship, snip, snip, went the rusty shears.

"Bald," wailed Dylan, eying his fallen locks.

"Fashionable." He bound Dylan's minimized hair with a fillet from the chest. "Now you look like Mercury."

"Who's he? A Merrow?"

"A god. Staff in his hand. Wings on his heels."

"I got webs."

"Just as good. Wears his hair like yours. Drawn behind his head. Crimson fillet."

"Oh, *that* god. Heard about him in the fleet. Guides ships in a storm. Brings you luck. Has a way wi' the lasses. Light fingers too. Bit piratical, though."

"Yes, but he never steals from the poor."

"If I'm Mercury, you're his twin. Learn my tricks from you. You're the naughty one, Nod." He gave his friend a quick, impulsive hug.

"Call us Castor and Pollux."

"Sounds like a poultice."

Dylan stared at his face, bordered, not forested, with his obsidian hair, in the looking glass, and grinned a piratical grin. "Might get to like it. But you know, I still don't un'erstand what to do at the festival. Wi' Stella and her friend. Corn Sprites. Fine ladies, both of 'em."

"Sweet-talk them."

"What's that?"

"You know. Compliment their gowns and jewels."

"Won't be wearin' any, will they, after the feastin'?"

"That's when you kiss."

"Mouth to mouth?"

"All over, I think."

"Uhmmmmm. Always did want a kiss on my ear. Then what?"

"And you a sailor?"

"Galley slave. Ain't the same. Chained up most o' the time. All we could do was talk. 'Cept that one time wi' the master's wife."

"What exactly did the two of you do?"

"Not much. Don't want to think about it. *She* wasn't no lady."

"Well, what did the other rowers talk about? I mean, some of them must have pleasured before they were galley slaves." He looked questioningly at Dylan, hopeful no doubt of a—Mercurial—answer.

Dylan scratched his head. Before his loss of hair, a scratch had been difficult, if not impossible. Now, he was careful to limit the length of his scratch, in case he should lose his remaining hair.

"Must've all right. Sure talked about it enough when they weren't rowin' or restin'. One of 'em said"—he paused. "Nod, not prissy, are you?"

"Dylan, I've told you I'm not a Christian."

"No matter. Still don't know how they talk, them in the galley. Thieves, boozers, wenchers. *Salty.* Used to make my ears tingle. And half the time I dinna know what they meant."

"I talk raunchy with my friends," confessed Nod (what he did not confess was his lack of friends). "Raunchy is much the same as salty, I expect. Let's face it. Both of us mean to be men of the world, and the world is as full of wenches as a hive with bees, or so I hear" (with every meal).

"Sure do like you, kid. Sheltered all your life, but ready to raise canvas and steer for the Pillars o' Hercules."

"Kid? I'm fifteen!"

"Lad. How's that?"

"How old can a lad be?"

"Up to twenty or so."

"That's all right then." An expectant pause. "You were going to tell me what you heard from the men."

"Somebody said: 'Man and woman built to fit. Key in a lock.' Seems kind o' silly, don't it? All that fuss about people bein' keys and locks."

"I think," said Nod, "that when you lock, that's when you pleasure. Haven't you felt a need to, um, open some doors?"

"Sure have. Felt like a regular thief at times. Door don't open, want to break it down."

"I don't think we will have to smash any doors. Not at Stella's festival."

"Had another feeling."

"What was that?"

"Can't hardly describe it. A woman like Stella, for instance. She makes a man feel like—like protectin', not breakin'. But I'd still want to use my key. Know what I mean?"

"Exactly. When you built your house, and the last piece was in place, how did you feel?"

"Like a kind o' god."

"It will be the same with Stella."

"How 'bout the dumb one?"

"I never said she was dumb."

"Didn't have to. Sounds like a sheep."

"Tutelina. You might call her—not very bright. We don't want to hurt her feelings, though, that's for sure. But she doesn't see too well. I think just about anybody can supply a key, and she won't even know the difference."

"Old woman?"

"She doesn't *look* old."

"Key's ready then. Galley slaves can't be choosers. How much longer?"

"Not long. I think the sun has set. The light's gone from the door."

"And Angus is hungry." He lit a candle from his smouldering hearth and filled a bowl with poppy seeds. "Here, Angus. Suppertime." Then to Nod. "Feed him an' maybe he won't follow us. Don't want him seein' his master act like old Mercury."

"Well then. Take off your cloak and let's get ready."

"Not goin' naked, are we? Had enough o' that in the galleys. Makes me want to blush, rememberin'."

"You've still got your loin cloth."

"That's downstairs. It's upstairs to worry about."

"Dylan, I think you've got things reversed. Anyway, Stella will set you straight."

Dylan frowned and touched his hand to a newly visible ear. "Think she'll want to? Got holes in my ears. Pierced, don't you think. Mark of a slave."

"Nod returned to the chest. "Here," he said.

"Earrings?"

"Black jade. Very precious. And these were made for a man. You can tell by the size of the rings."

"Feel like a flozy."

"Floozy."

"Same thing. One o' the words I learnt in the fleet. Woman who paints her face and uses henna to dye hair instead of walls o' a house."

"You don't look like a floozy, you look like an Etruscan prince. You'll be the lord of the festival."

Dylan, Roman practicality warring with Celtic fancy, breathed a sorrowful sigh. "Sure. Till the pleasurin' comes. Sounds like work."

"Don't worry. Leave everything to Stella."

"Leavin' a lot to her, aren't we? Won't have eyes for a Roane, that's for sure."

"I think," said Nod, none too happily, "that she may have eyes for both of us. That seems to be the way of these festivals."

"Ought to hide them shoulders, Nod. Might embarrass her and give me the edge after all."

Arm in arm, they went to the festival.

★ Chapter Seven ★

The wheat ahead of them was as high as a man, a muted bronze in the light of a harvest moon, and Dylan blinked before he could see the people among the stalks.

"Whole town's turned out," he muttered. "Might recognize me." He looked at Nod, whose hair, unfilleted, covered his ears (*pity. Ears ought to show*) but fell in little golden clusters over his forehead and framed his head; the large green eyes; the blond brows with mischievous upturned ends, the white, strong teeth (*'cept one's a bit crooked*). The minor imperfection inordinately pleased him. In one way, at least, he, imperfect Dylan, surpassed his paragon. (*Ain't pretty, that boy, but almost. Comely. That's the word. Makes me look like a sun-baked Nubian. He'll get Stella all right. I'll get the squinty one*).

With a start, he saw that the moonlight concealed the actual color of eyes and hair. Already, it seemed, he had memorized Nod's features; he had only to look at the lad, in a cave, under the moon, in total darkness, and the colors, the configuration, leaped into place.

Nod laughed the happy, reverberating laugh of a boy with a friend on the verge of an expedition. "Dylan, remember the looking glass." (*Nod, bronze in the moonlight. More than human?*)

"Brought the old me back again, did it?"

"Nobody will recognize you for Cedalion, the Beast Man."

She came to them through the fields and Dylan wanted to kneel at her feet and kiss her sandal straps. Had she come from the moon, whose beneficent beams encouraged the stalks of wheat to reach toward its luminous face? The sun was often inimical; hot and withering; the moon was perpetual nurturer whenever it shone, and tonight it shone in the fulness of its power.

And what of Stella, woven of moonbeams and air? No, she was also of earth; wind in her hair but hair like tassels of wheat ... soft ... soft ... as if it were woven instead of grown. And the gown she wore ... it was less a gown than a revelation. He had never seen the form of a beautiful woman. He had never seen divinity in the flesh. Ant hills? Melons? Sailors' talk! Comparisons failed him before the incomparable.

"Nod!" she cried. "I was afraid for you."

"I lost the cheese and bread. A demoness chased me, and I never got the wine!"

"Dearest friend, were you hurt in your flight?"

"No, she really did me a favor. She chased me to *him*. He's my friend. Cedalion. Only his name is really Dylan. Remember, you saw him on the hill."

"Well, you shall meet no demons tonight, not the inimical kind, at least. The rustics have brought me wine, flour, honey, and olive oil, and I have mixed them to please the gods."

Dylan felt her gaze, a scrutiny almost tangible, like fingers of sprouting grass. *Knows things but not tellin'. Where I come from to start wi'. Not Caledonia. 'Fore that. Knows my mother? Why she left me wi' out a word?*

She laughed and took his hand. "Cedalion! Why, you're only a boy."

"Been around, ma'am."

"I know," she said, laughter subsiding into a smile; the smile wistful, compassionate. "I meant in years, not experience. I can see the voyages in your eyes, the hurt, the despair. But tonight is a different voyage, and not into pain. May I be your pilot?"

"P-pilot?" he stammered, further speech eluding him.

"Guide. Belovéd, if you will."

"Sweet-talk her," whispered Nod. "It's expected."

"Ain't ant hills," he blurted, eying the green transparency of her gown. "Better."

"You have paid me a princely compliment," she said, turning his clumsy words into a paean. "My Nod has found himself a worthy friend." Then, giving each of the boys an arm, she led them through trellises weighted with swollen grapes; among olive trees, glinting like cornucopias heaped with coins; into the wheat and the heart of the festival. The scent of grapes was muscatel in the air; the olive and wheat, earth's own ambrosial feast. Olympus, thought Dylan, remembering ancient stories by ancient men in the galleys, of gods and heroes, of valor and cunning, of high-walled cities and queens whose beauty inspired men to build or raze them, the goddesses loving mortals and siring immortal sons. Now was then, and then was the time of the gods, and not of the god who was jealous and cruel, born of the deserts and, like them, despising women, and woman's compassionate ways. Then was Stella. . . .

Now was Stella.

"Tutelina," she called. "I have found another devotee!" Dylan balked in his tracks, reclaiming his hand; bear-stubborn, bear-immovable. After a goddess, a jester? Nod's description had hardly exalted her.

Her motion was that of a ship avoiding shoals. She paused to greet a cluster of wheat stalks which she mistook for men.

"Forgive me, Sirs, I have made commitments. Perhaps later." Then, imminently before collision, she recognized Nod.

"Nod, my dear, who is your fetching friend?"

"Dylan. From Caledonia."

"Dylan, I bid you welcome to our festival."

Beaming, blinking, she was impossible to dislike. Surprisingly in fact, he liked her at once: the look of her, rounded but not fat; plenty amidst the plentiful fields. To him she was much more than a beauteous, nearsighted young woman over-eager to please. She was what Caledonia needed to make it hospitable; the lush green palms of the south which should have companioned the solitary oak. Stella and Tutelina were both of the earth, but Stella was goddess, Tutelina woman. With Stella, he felt in awe; with Tutelina, at ease.

"Oh, Stella, Stella, what a feast we shall have! How the

fields will flourish!" She peered into Dylan's face. "Have you ever seen such teeth? And look at those brawny arms! You must have wielded a spear against the Gauls.

"Rowed a galley, ma'am."

"My poor boy," she said. "They can be very cruel, the men who rule this land. They have forgotten the old kindnesses." She bent toward him to plant a kiss on his cheek but hit his ear. "Oh, goodness, may I try again?"

"Like bein' kissed on the ear. Best place I know."

She kissed him crookedly on the nose.

"Better the first time. Want to try again?"

"It's her age," whispered Stella. "But don't let on. She's terribly sensitive about such things."

"Is it time for the orgy?" inquired Nod, edging away from Tutelina and fixing his sights on Stella, as a mariner takes a fix on the North Star.

"First we must greet our guests," said Stella, smiling but adamant. Dylan thought with a start: She is woven of moonbeams, but the earth in her is bronze.

At least a hundred pagans from Misna and the outlying farms and even a score of Christians, looking about them with a furtive air, hoping not to be recognized by their neighbors, had come to the festival. The men wore loin cloths; young, most of them, muscular without being brawny from their gymnasia; proud to display their shoulders and chests in a time when men were accustomed to wearing togas in public; a few of them rustics and rusty from the sun; all of them ogling the women in such a way to suggest a key in search of a lock.

The ladies had not worn cloaks above their ankle-length stolas or tunics. It was unusual, it was usually unthinkable, for a Roman lady to leave her cloak in the house, but the air had a special feel, a warmth, a communion which seemed to say, "This is a night to forget the new modesty of Rome, the Empire, Rome turning toward Christ, and remember the old liberty when the Fauns and the Dryads frolicked under the moon." Their stolas were clasped above their shoulders with insect pins in silver or gold—butterfly, hawk moth, grasshopper—but the clasps looked eminently breakable, a butterfly poised for flight, a grasshopper tensed to jump. A sudden tug, a twist, an intricate step in a dance ... Dylan, unaware of a third, tight-fitting garment against a lady's body, fancied a prod to every clasp; a deluge of sliding stolas; a garden of naked women flaunting their melons and copses for the agile gardener.

He felt a familiar but unidentifiable sensation: a heat in his loins leaping out of control and suffusing every limb. He had felt it in fact when the friendly Romans had told him the nature of girls. Being a Roane and a Celt, he could not confine himself to a single image; not at such a time. Keys and gardens awhirl in his brain, a fire consuming his limbs, would barely suffice to describe his confusion of feelings, his expectation and his apprehension.

"Stella," he said. "Chosen me, have you?"

"Patience," she said, more to the crowd than to him. "The Lady Moon must climb the hill of the heavens to oversee our feast."

He heard them argue with Stella and then among themselves. His elongated ears could distinguish the separate voices.

A Roman gallant to a coy girl: "Saw you coming from the basilica only yesterday. What are you doing *here?*"

The coy girl, gowned in a stola which, even by moonlight, showed her body in its multiple splendors: "I believe in the One True God. But before him were other gods, Ceres and Liber, Fannus, and Luperca. Perhaps, if any are left, they will welcome our sacrifice."

"You don't fool me, my dear. You didn't come to worship."

"Hush! The wheat has ears. It might catch fire."

A rustic in the afterthought of a loin cloth: "Wheat's got *tassels,* not ears."

"Stella," said Nod. "Do you think we could skip the feast? I suspect the Lady Moon has already spied Endymion."

Endymion ... the sleepy fellow. Loved by the Moon, notwi'standin'. Always had a way wi words, that Nod. Might be a Celt. Right too. I'm a—conflagration!

"Nod."

"Yes, Stella?"

"Listen. What do you hear?"

"Shouting," he said. "Everybody's shouting. Loudly, too."

"Under the loudness."

"Do you mean the wind in the wheat?"

"Softer still."

"You mean. . . ."

Suddenly Dylan thought: Nod knows.

What?

The meaning of the festival. How a garden of girls can be the same as a field of wheat. Needing a similar bounty of sun and rain. How to bestow such a bounty.

Nod knew. Kneeling, he clasped his arms around the thin, jointed stalks which rose into rounded tassels and silken threads.

"Dizzy, lad?" asked Dylan.

"No," whispered Nod. "I'm trying to talk. . . ."

"Sure you are. To me and Stella." He knelt beside his friend.

"To the wheat." Nod confronted him with the look of a god intoxicated by prayer: Bonus Eventus, clay become flesh.

Dylan shook his head. " 'Bout what?"

"Oh, it isn't words exactly. The wheat is—lonely."

"Like Angus, when he wants to be petted?"

"In a different way. It's going to be scythed and turned into bread, and it wants to know why."

"Don't know what to say."

"Neither do I." Bonus Eventus had fled from him, leaving a baffled boy.

"To the gods," said Stella, "silence can be as rare a gift as words. Is the wheat not a goddess?" She leaned above them, amber and gold . . . amber and gold. Moon—begotten, earth—born. Deity, woman, lover. Extending her hands as if in a benediction, she lifted them to their feet with equal ease, though Dylan was heavier by a stone than Nod. "First we must eat the sacrificial meal. Tutelina, help me. . . ."

Stella and Tutelina passed among the crowd, spreading

wine in tiny, bee-shaped vessels and honey cakes plump
as sparrows. A galley slave, Dylan had tasted wines in
many lands, all of them cheap, most of them sharp or
sour. Warm water, stale bread, and cheap wine: These
had been the staples of his diet. Now, he longed for a
sea-cow's milk or the sweet juice of the grapes which had
nurtured him in his cave.

Until he tasted the wine:

Gingerly, expecting the rancid beverages from the galleys, murky red or mottled white, bitter with flotsam and
jetsam of cork and dirt and perhaps an occasional worm
which had crept from the ancient bread. He took a second
taste, smacked his lips, felt an agreeable radiance in his
stomach, admired the roseate hue, and emptied the flagon
in one quick gulp.

"Got another, Stella?"

"Another?" smiled Stella. "You'll be drunk before the
orgy! Eat some honey cakes."

He had never been drunk in all of his sixteen years; the
wine in the fleet had been doled in swallows, and rarely,
to revive the strength of the rowers.

"Like it," he said.

"Do you, Dylan?"

"Love you."

"Because of the wine."

"No!" Love was at once a simplicity and complexity
which needed no explanation. To describe meant to pro-
scribe, like building a wall around an acropolis. A wall
excluded friends as well as thieves.

"Listen, Dylan," said Nod. "Stella has started the rit-
ual."

She spoke but she seemed to sing:

The Great Mother folded her wonder of wings and
leaned above the world. Her tears fell as rain but they did
not moisten the fields nor fill the river beds, parched with
midsummer, remembering spring's sweet snows.

"He has wooed me," she said. "He has asked me to be
his queen. But his ways are cruel. He has cast the pall of

his cruelty across the world. The temples are hushed. The holy fires have been quenched by water and ashes, the rites have been scattered on alien winds."

And Stella sang:

The Gods Abide

The old gods never die,
The gods abide
Out of the heaven's blonde, unblinking eye.
In oak or elm or fir
(Still . . . mouse-in-a-hayrick still):
Under the hill,
Bereft of priest and feast,
Of temples redolent with nard and myrrh
(God is a hooded viper . . . hide, hide):
Under the halcyon meadows of the sea,
Most is least,
Wings are folded, flight is memory.

The gods abide.

God is a hooded viper? Which god, he wondered . . . Jupiter . . . Neptune . . . Mars? The Olympians forced to hide in the sea or under a hill? Mercury folding his wings? Temples and priests abounded in Misna and other towns, and Stella's feast was surely a festival. Nothing had fled from the world, so far as he knew, neither light nor music nor magic nor deity. Indeed, Nod could talk to the wheat and Stella was beautiful.

Perhaps the song was a prophecy and a warning.

Silence lay like a flaxen toga over the fields. Everyone looked to Stella, the men of the town, the girls, the farmers, Nod. Dylan saw them at first as a faceless crowd; then the faces separated themselves like anemones in the undersea gardens of Caledonia: the rustic, stooped and weathered in spite of his youth; the haughty patrician, humbled for the night; the coy girl, willing for once to trade fashion for fun. He saw the many, he saw the one.

G. Barr

He saw them discard their robes and their shame and
stand enrobed and ennobled in a primal innocence.

"Now" cried Stella, tossing her head, shaking her
treasure of moondusted hair. "We shall conjure them out
of hiding!"

Archaic presences whispered among the wheat. He was
afraid of them. And her. He tried to shut his eyes; magicked, he had to cover them with his hands.

Nod removed the hands. "Dylan, there isn't any shame
in the naked body."

"Not below," said Dylan, remembering Caledonia and
the cold, bracing sea around his loins. *"Above."*

"Only the Christians hide the glory of womanhood."

Dylan removed his loin cloth with some reluctance.

"Cloak too."

"Must?"

"Must."

He shivered but not from the chill in the air. He shrank
among the wheat and hoped that the stalks would hide his
shoulders' loss.

Nod did not even try to hide his nakedness. He stood
in the lucid amber of the moon and Bonus Eventus had
returned to him.

"Thought you was new to the festival."

"Stella makes the difference, don't you see?"

She flickered toward them, smiling her eldritch smile.

"Take Nod," he begged, desperate in his nudity. "I got
gills and webbed feet!" What did he know of queens or
goddesses?

"Dylan, I have come for *you.*"

"Not for me?" cried Nod. He looked like a little boy
whose goatcart had overturned and lost a wheel.

"Trade you," whispered Dylan. "Even take Tutelina."

"Dearest Nod," said Stella. "For you and me there
must be another love. For we are kin."

"Bloodkin?"

"Born of the earth,'" she said, "and not the sea. Look!
Tutelina, our cousin, is coming to meet us."

"If you're my kin, so's she," said Nod. "I don't want

her. She means well, I know, but she's—well, a bit simple, isn't she?"

"Nod, you are very young. Tutelina is shy."

"Yes, like a Harpy."

"She needs your love."

"And you don't?"

"In a different way. Go to her now."

Roseate and delectable, a sheared young sheep but meant for the table and not the couch, so he thought, she stumbled toward them across the fields.

"Would you scorn her on such a night?"

Well, it was good to be needed, even by a sheep. "Whatever you say. But may I have one of the girls from Misna too? After Tutelina, I mean. Dessert, as it were. Duty first, then pleasure. Really, I have a great deal of catching up to do. Fifteen years of chastity! Can you imagine what I have missed?"

"My little virgin! Become a Hercules, if you like. But always—tenderness. Sacredness. Affirmation in the order of things, the intricate, admirable, unfathomable design of thhe Great Mother, and the God behind the gods."

"Well then, I think I'll get on with the affirmation. I suppose you're going to affirm with Dylan?"

"Am I, Dylan?" Goddesses did not usually ask; for the moment, at least, she was less a deity than a suppliant.

"Yea," said Dylan, surprising himself with the promptness of his reply. "But I . . . I . . . got them holes in my ears. Ain't pretty. Marks of a slave, you see.

"The earrings hide them."

"Look like a girl."

"A prince of Etruria."

"That's what Nod said."

"Nod is a loyal friend. Trust him. Love him."

"Guess I already do. But your kind o' love—harder. Don't know how to start."

"Mine must be learned, like planting a crop in the right season or field. But I am a patient teacher." She took his hand and pressed it against her cheek.

"Smell like a flower, ma'am."

"Narcissus. I wear a pouch of petals between my
breasts. They bring me luck."

"Don't need it."

"Everyone does. I with you, it seems. Am I strange to
your touch, my dear?"

"Nay," he cried and jerked her to him and, in spite of
himself, kissed her bruisingly on the mouth.

"Softly. Love is like wine. It must be sipped and sa-
vored. You emptied your cup too fast. Will you do the
same with love?"

"Sober now. Able to savor." His wine-befuddled senses
leaped into clarity.

"Follow me then!"

She led him into a dance, a slow swaying movement
among the wheat, quickening, leaping into a whirl instead
of a sway, and who were the other dancers and which was
the wheat, he could not say, and now they were one, he
and she and the dance, they and the wheat, and the earth
in its aerial journey through the ether... Drunk but not
with wine, he trod the ground like a rustic at the vintage,
and yet he did not feel the earth, the roots, the fallen
stalks of wheat; it was air he trod, and with Mercury's
wingéd heels.

The fire from his loins made him a leaping torch.

"Stella!" he cried and crouched at her feet, the child he
had been when memory fell upon him like a woven net
whose warp was loss and whose woof was loneliness.

"Dearest Dylan," she said. "Are you afraid of me?"

"Not you, ma'am. Dance made me dizzy."

"It wasn't the dance, Dylan, was it? With me you must
always speak the truth."

"Don't know what."

"You haven't known many women, have you?"

"None in Caledonia. Nearest thing to a woman was a
seal. Myself, never took to 'em 'cept as friends. Then the
galleys, and a somethin' called a flozy. Then the cave.
Demoness thereabouts. Worse than a Shelleycoat!"

"I must be a terror to you then, my dear. I must seem
a threat instead of a lure."

"Threat? A bloody wonder, that's what you are! And me a' ill-favored fisher lad. That's why I'm scared."

"Listen to me, belovéd. Wonder is—distance, strangeness, mystery. It is another kingdom. Sphinxes to guard the border. Towers against the horizon, seemingly unclimbable. Gardens of moonflowers and moonlit swallows, but shut behind walls and gates. At first you must tiptoe, at first you must whisper. Know, whatever, that you are beautiful. *And beauty opens the gate.*"

"Razor helped. Nod said it would."

"Your heart looks out of your eyes. What I see I love."

Gently, gently she moved, spoke, at once released and encompassed him. (Where had she learned her gentleness? From dolphins under the sea or halcyons in the air?)

"Will you kiss my ear, ma'am?"

"Your ears might have come from the sea. The exquisite convolutions—they remind me of murex shells."

"Hear good too."

"How not?"

"Moonflower," he murmured. "That's what you are, Stella." At last he had managed to speak her name with ease. "But warm like a sunflower at noon."

"As good as cold?"

"Never like cold again."

"Kneel with me then," she said. "Place an ear on the ground. What do you hear?"

"Sound o' feet."

"Under the feet."

"Growin' things. Roots strugglin' to reach the sun."

"What do they say to you?"

"Have to ask Nod."

"Answer for yourself."

"Dylan, Dylan, Dylan. Seem to be sayin' my name. Askin'."

"Asking what?"

"What you can tell me."

He did not feel the kiss on the lobe of his ear. He felt the kiss in the nest of his heart, like a swallow with folded wings, soft, silent, settling into rest. If he could keep it but not in prison. If he could nurture it, feed it, never break its wings. . . .

First, shame fell from him like a sealskin cloak; then, naked in spirit as well as body, tiptoeing, striding, he crossed the borders into the kingdom of love.

"Dylan, Dylan, Dylan," sang the wheat (or was it Stella?). Replenished. Grateful. Quiescent.

He crouched apart from her and began to weep.

She gathered him to her breast, she the golden, she the goddess.

"Never mind, little one. You have given your seed."

"Gone," he said. "No more gifts for you."

"It is often the way of love. After joy, sadness. After harvesting, snow. But seedtime follows the frost . . . inexorably."

"Never cried when they whipped me. Shouldn't from love." (But Nod had cried in the cave.)

"Shouldn't you, Dylan? Weep, my dear. Weep against Stella's breast, but not like a little boy. Shall I sing to you?"

"Yea."

"Beast, beast,
Fierce with fear,
Fear love least;
Lay your head,
Shaggy, in my arms' quiet bed.
Sleep, my dear."

"Goin' to lie wi' somebody else now?"

"I am the queen of the festival."

"Queen can do or not."

"Love divided is like the loaves of bread in the Christian parable. Give them to those in need, and then they multiply."

"Ain't a Christian."

"But Christ was the son of a god, and what he taught was wise and true. It is his followers—Paul and some of

the rest—who have forgotten the truth. It is they who de-
fame the Mother."

"Dinna come for a sermon."

"No more sermons," she laughed.

"Canna go."

"I must."

"Want to?"

She looked at him with surprise and puzzlement. "Why,
yes. It has always been my way."

"Wish we'd never met," he barked. "Don't want nobody else nibblin' my loaf."

It was then that he smelled the smoke. It was then that
he felt a heat which was not of love.

★ Chapter Eight ★

"Love-making," said Tutelina, "is not to be judged by the speed of its execution."

It was her first intelligent remark in the course of their affirmation. Indeed, it was her only remark. Till now she had held her tongue and withheld advice, and Nod had been forced to improvise like a man of the world. Instinct, together with episodes heard in the markets and barbershops of Misna, had been his guide. In theory, he knew that the key must fit the lock; the size of his key was a source of pride to him, and the consummation, achieved, so he thought, with commendable speed, was at once a release and a pleasure which he assumed to be shared by Tutelina. If it was not exactly an exaltation, if it was, in fact, a minor disappointment after his long and arduous virginity, he blamed his inexperience and Tutelina's indifference and had no doubt that he would improve with practice and a change of partners.

"I forgot the sweet-talking, didn't I?" he said. "But we wasted all that time eating and drinking. It's going to be sunrise before we know it." Around him, the few visible couples gave no immediate promise of division. "Shall we. . . ?"

Tutelina blinked; it was only the blink which recalled the foolish young woman thrust upon him by her solicitous friend. She did not speak like a fool.

"Of course you wanted Stella instead of me. Or one of those bumptious girls from Misna. I was charity. I was to be dispatched and replaced with the speed of rape. Rape, to be sure, has its proper place. Take Cassandra, for instance. She made an art of teasing and Ajax called her bluff. But under the present circumstances. . . ."

Nod had never disliked Tutelina, in spite of her ovine ways (even a sheep is good for wool); now, he began to respect her. Certainly he did not want to wound her pride.

"But I offered a—well, an adequate tool, did I not? My friends call him Lordon because he is—"

"More than adequate. Prodigious for one so young. Of course it goes with your race."

Prodigious. . . . the word had implications beyond number, all of them delectable. Virile, phallic, Priapic . . . terms which, anathema to Christians, were natural and even enviable to pagans, who placed Priapus' statue amidst their gardens and in their bedrooms. He had often exercised nude in the gymnasia and, in the fashion of boys, compared endowments. The boys had admired him and named his manhood "Lordon," after his tutelary god, Priapus' son.

"What more do you want?" he protested. "And I asked you a second time."

"That was after I proved—satisfactory—the first time. And after you saw the lack of a ready replacement. I have no quarrel with London. But you must learn to deserve him." Her eyes ceased to flutter and he realized that, at such a range, she saw him with absolute clarity, and also *into* him. No longer did she resemble a rubicund sheep. Plumpness was amplitude, then desirability. Her sudden lack of a smile reminded him that its previous presence had concealed—what?—hurts, losses, perhaps even anguishes; most of all, time. "In short, you wanted Stella."

"Yes," he admitted. "She stirred me from the first, how I don't understand. I thought it must be for Lordon's sake. Now I think it was for something else. All I know is that I felt an immediate—affinity."

"Thank you for telling me the truth." She recovered her smile and kissed him on the cheek; at least, she aimed for the cheek but met his chin. Still, the warmth of the gesture did not escape him. "I know, sweet Nod. And I am—well, a talkative old woman with—with"—the words came hard for her—"diminished vision."

"I think you see just fine," he blurted, pondering the 'old woman.' "The important things, anyway."

"Do you, Nod?"

"I'm the nearsighted one. But how am I kin to Stella?"

"She will tell you in time."

"Meanwhile, will you give Lordon and me another chance?"

"Gladly. And don't reproach yourself for your original, uh, pounce. Love is a gift but even a gift must be perfected. And you a *virgin* at that." (She might have been a Christian uttering "whore"). "I think you have made a tolerable beginning."

"Tolerable? Let's start from the first. And you be my guide. You have already complimented my friend. In other words, I have the wherewithal. It must be my *use* that's at fault."

"Love, my dear, is prodigality of the soul, though the wherewithal, I will have to admit, is not without his charm. Sweet-talk me."

"Tutelina, I think you are as delectable as a honey comb to a hungry bear."

"Excellent. I have a taste for sweets and a partiality for bears. In exchange, may I say that your limbs are a graceful mixture of smoothness and muscularity. And as for your face—Bonus Eventus might envy those green, incredible eyes. I can see their color even by moonlight, you understand. Like emeralds, they never change color. As for Lordon, well, what can I say? He does his father proud."

"My cheeks are too plump."

"Not for a corn Sprite."

"Am I?"

"Didn't you say you were?" she evaded.

"Hoped I was. They seem to have such fun."

"Had. Now you may kiss me on the neck. No, no, Nod, I didn't say bite. You aren't a blood-sucking Strige. Now you may use your tongue. Foolish boy. Not a lick!"

"But I'm a hungry bear."

"You're right, metamorphoses are the spice of love. Look to Jove for example. Snake. Bull. Swan. But *never* a bear. Whatever suited the lady."

"And fooled his wife." Worldly Nod! After tonight he and Dylan could wench in the sporting houses and pass for masters.

"At the moment, you are a delicate sunbird sipping

nectar. Perfect. Now you may ease your way down the mountain range. Imagine yourself a sure-footed goat. And don't neglect the foothills to the rear."

"Tutelina," he said as he started to ease, "may I spend the entire festival exploring your geography?"

"Have you the stamina for such an extended journey?" Then, eying Lordon, "Yes, of course you have. I keep forgetting your race. I am honored, my dear, and you are improving with every kiss. You haven't drawn blood since the first. But the fields enjoy a—how do I say?—mingling of devotees. Quantity pleased them as well as quality."

"But the wheat is grown! It's waiting to be harvested. Isn't this a harvest festival?"

"Tonight we are thanking the earth for what she has already given us and insuring a repetition of the gift. She receives our emanations of joy—and rejoices. She drinks of the man's sweet nectar and stores it against the winter sleep; imprints the woman's body in earthen lineaments and feels vicarious shudders of pelasure and love. There are other festivals—one for the ploughing, one for the planting—when we thank her for what she promises to give."

"Do you think I've learned enough to mingle?"

"You have conquered the mountains. Why not attempt the valley?"

"As a goat?"

"As a young bull."

I'm a bloody circus, he thought, borrowing an oath from Dylan.

But every beast was fed. . . .

"Tutelina," he smiled, master of mountain and valley. Prodigal as well as prodigious. "You aren't at *all* stupid."

"People generally think me so," she sighed. "I have a way of, well, bumbling. You could call it age, but then I was always a bumbler. At the age of eleven I wandered into a cave of Fauns, mistaking it for a Dryad's tree. I was just in time for dessert."

"I'm sure you were better than sweet meats or honey cakes."

"Forgive my boast, but every Faun took a second serving."

"And you aren't plump either. Every roundness is in the proper place. Especially mountains and foothills."

"Hush, my dear, you will make me blush."

A black bulbous head waggled above them.

"A Telchin," sighed Tutelina. "Excellent workers but terrible prudes. *Monogamous.* I thought they were extinct."

"This one is named Angus," explained Nod, "and he's probably looking for Dylan." He shook his head and assumed a look of reproof.

Angus scuttled among the wheat stalks to pursue his search.

"Really, he ought to be Christian," said Tutelina. "Those disapproving eyes. The *size* of his eyes. What was the question you asked me before the interruption?"

"I said, how about—?"

"Climb to your feet, boy!"

The voice was harsh and commanding; the speaker, muffled in tunic and toga but armed with a stave which might have routed a Sphinx, loomed above them like Moses descending Sinai.

"Sir," said Tutelina, "if you will lower your voice and lay aside your robe, I will try to accomodate you."

"It's my father," sighed Nod. "He isn't accomodative."

Marcus had brought his friends—a hundred Christians or more—to invade the fields with torches and staves and the armor of righteous arrogance. Lost in their explorations, Tutelina and Nod had failed to hear them approach. Now they could hear the knocking of wood against heads; the squeal of the maiden dragged from her lover's arms; the cry of a dandy with neither weapon nor garment; the gutteral curse of a rustic to rival a sailor's salt. Rob a man of his robes, thought Nod, and he runs to love but away from war or trade; in short, he hides. It was part of the new modesty; the Christians had given it a more specific name: Original Sin.

Marcus' fist, both knotted and unexpected, leveled the rising Nod. Spreadeagled on the ground, scent, sound, sight evaporating into oblivion, he somehow heard his father's final command. "Go home when you come to your senses. Or go to Hell. It's all the same to me."

Dimly Nod saw Tutelina grasped by the arm and jerked away from him and heard his father sneer. "And you, you whore of Babylon. How would you like to hang from a cross?"

"Let her go," gasped Nod. "Let her go—" Helpless, hapless, hopeless Tutelina! His tongue seemed stuck in his throat. I am suffocating, he thought. I am falling into Hell.

He fell into dreams. Devils danced in his brain (Christian) and prodded him with their pitchforks and shrilled in his ear: "That is for dancing under the moon with the whores of Babylon." Crucifixes forested his horizon; a hooded viper slithered between his feet; the unblinking eye of the sun stared imprecation and condemnation. . . .

He felt a gentle but persistent prod. Pitchforks. No, Angus' feelers. He climbed into consciousness and stared groggily around him, dislodging night-mares even as he awoke to pain, and saw the crowd had dispersed from the fields.

He had never expected to hug an ant. "Angus, old man, we've got to find Dylan and rescue the ladies." Angus appeared to understand the request. Staunchly the feelers stood him on his feet, held him in place till he recovered his balance, and nudged him into their mutual search.

Most of the ladies had forsaken their cloaks; some, their tunics and sandals and jewels and even head-dresses masquerading as hair. Loin cloths littered the ground like pieces of wash which a slave had left to dry. When naked love-makers are surprised by militant Christians, Mars and not Venus is certain to win the day. At least he could find no bodies; but then the Christians of Misna scarcely outnumbered the pagans and, with Constantine leaning but not committed to God, could not risk a final confrontation; furthermore, many of them resembled his mother, true to gentle Christ, who had said to the Magdalene, "Arise and sin no more"; suspicious of unforgiving Paul, who had characterized marriage as an antidote to lust.

But Stella's festival was a ruin and a screaming of crows. The wheat was broken and trampled, the trellised grapes uprooted and flung to the hungry birds; the gods had been descrated instead of consecrated (Ceres only knew what the fields would sprout. Probably tares). Even the moon had fled below the horizon to hide with Endymion, and lurid dawn besported in her place (red, not rosy-fingered, he thought).

Alone. . . .

Alone in the ruins, without his friends (where were his friends? Fled? Hurt? Captured?).

No, Angus had come to keep him company. He patted a rounded flank and a reassuring feeler flicked his ear and pointed, unmistakably, to the summer house where he had been found as a child. Snatching a loin cloth from the ground, he softly threaded his way among the broken wheat and the trampled trellises. The cloth felt damp and tight around his loins; a tunic would have encased him like a breastplace. (Something had fled from the free and open fields; something had fled behind the walls of the town. *Once he had seen a nightingale in a wicker cage. The bird had forgotten to sing.*)

The blankness which follows surprise, pain, oblivion had yielded to tentative plans. He could not return to Misna, of that he was sure. His mother, being a Christian, was not in danger. Companioned by Angus, he would rescue his friends, Dylan, Stella, and Tutelina, and ride in the orange-hooded pilentum to the north, where the Christian mildew had yet to spread and taint the countryside and sicken the people. Or sail in Dylan's boat to the Misty Isles. He would miss his mother, miss her dreadfully—the plainness of her which was a kind of beauty, the courage of her which dared to deceive and defy his father; the softness, sweetness, gentleness—but he was readier now to find and depart with his friends than return to a home which harbored a man like Marcus.

To find the depart with his friends. . . .

He had underestimated the weaponry of the peace-proclaiming Christians. Or rather, he underestimated his father, who, with the dormouse-bottomed priest, was raising a hastily hammered cross behind the summer house. Twenty men at the least, Christian of course, were watching the operation or holding to Tutelina. Naked except for her dishevelment of hair, a curiously becoming garment, she looked more indignant than frightened, and eager to fight instead of bumble.

"Fetch some nails," shouted his father.

"Iron," added the priest, when Tutelina bit him on the arm.

I am to blame, thought Nod. Dylan and Stella may have fled to the wagon, but Tutelina, escaping from my father, probably mistook the Christians for hayricks and blundered into their midst.

If Tutelina was angry, Nod was outraged, as much with himself as with the Christians. At the time of his capture, she had been his woman, his affirmation; he had failed her and, irony of ironies, through the machinations of his own father.

But what he felt was more complicated than anger; it was also the threat of losing someone whom he had taken to be a clown and come to respect as a woman; and even more important, the threat to *her,* the indignity, the pain, the possible death.

The possible death. . . Anger clawed his throat like the roots of the hellebore.

Forgetting Angus, he rose to his full height among the trellises; he snatched a wooden stake, sprang from concealment, and opened his mouth to remind those so-called Christians that even woman-hating Paul had never murdered a woman (had he?).

He felt a hand at his mouth and a tug at his loin cloth: Dylan, Stella beside him. He wanted to shout and laugh at the same time. He wanted to be a dolphin and wrestle with Dylan under the waves. He wanted to be a hayrick and feel the blesséd, blessing hand of Stella in benediction. How had he come so quickly to love two strangers as more than friends? Brother and sister, they seemed, the dark and the gold.

He embraced the two of them in one gigantic hug even as they dragged him into their viny escape; felt the warmth of their bodies; gathered the warmth against the cold to come. Dylan pulled his ear; Stella kissed his cheek. Passionate friendship; love beatified into a sacrament.

"Angus!" he cried. "We've found them! Now we can save Tutelina."

Angus' feelers flashed like ebony swords. Adoration glittered in his eyes (multiple adorations? Master and master's friend and *her,* whom he somehow seemed to know?).

"No," whispered Stella. Whisper was command. "You stay here, the two of you with your Telchin. I'll go."

"You! Alone?"

"Lower your voice, Nod. Yes. I'll distract them while you and Dylan see to Tutelina." He missed the gentleness of her; he feared the sudden strength. She looked so intent—perhaps indomitable was the word—that she seemed to be bearing a shield like an Amazon.

"Lass's goin' to war," grinned Dylan.

"But she's a woman!"

"Woman's a' admiral, laddie! Should've seen her crack skulls! One sight o' her, and Auld Hornie hisself would tuck his tail and run."

"But Stella," wailed Nod. "You're naked. They'll crucify you like Tuteline and gape at your mountains and valleys. Or tear you limb from limb. Or both. Look at them now, with Tutelina, who doesn't have half the what have you that you have."

"Christians are only men," said Stella. "Even your father. And Venus is still a goddess, whatever they think."

"But that's just it. Your beauty will drive them into a frenzy."

"Frenzied men are foolish warriors."

"You don't even have a weapon."

"You have a stake. Dylan has a stave. I don't need a weapon. I am the bait."

She walked toward the summer house as determinedly as a young wife on her way to an assignation.

Dylan, who had somehow acquired a cloak, though his netherlands remained superbly nude, threw a protective arm around his friend. "Ever see anythin' like it, lad? Makes you feel like worshippin'."

The Christians did not, it appeared, feel like worship or, for that matter, crucifixion. At first they stared. Then they gaped. Then they howled, like a pride of lions in pursuit of an edible oryx.

"Will you kindly release my friend?" she asked in firm but feminine tones.

"It's the other Sprite," said Marcus, addressing the priest but staring at naked Stella. "The dangerous one."

"Not going to crucify *her*," said a little fellow with downturned ears and outthrusting stave.

"Why not?"

"Think of the waste! Besides, if she fructifies the fields, what's the harm. It saves us fertilizer and irrigation. Just might help her in fact."

"Fornicator!" Marcus to Stella.

"Adulteress!" The priest, removing his toga to free himself for a chase.

"Lost my stave," said the little man with downturned ears. "Such a waste."

With the air of consuls marching against the Gauls, the priest and Marcus strode to meet the Sprite; then, before they met, she turned and, Hippolyte-swift, vanished among the arbors.

"After her!" shouted Marcus.

"After her!" shouted the priest, though Nod suspected the crucifixion had slipped his mind. "Not everybody! You, and you, and you. Guard the first one."

Tutelina's guard was reduced from an army of crucifiers to three old men who stared with obvious envy after the chase and the chased.

"Know how to use a stake?" whispered Dylan to Nod.

"Aim it for the nearest head."

No one saw them till they poised to aim. Tutelina, finding a rusty hoe, joined the fray.

The battle was instantaneous; the victory predictable. Tutelina aimed for a man with a beard and hit a man who was bald; Dylan hit the beard; and Nod was left to dispatch the remaining foe, whose cheeks were as hairless as his head.

A total rout.

"Now we'll find Stella and go to my cave," said Dylan.

"Won't they follow us?"

"Not to Cedalion's lair. Folk keep away from the bristly beast. Hey, laddie, where's Angus?"

"He must have followed Stella."

"She don't even know him."

"Dylan, I think she does. I think he went to help her."

"And now we're back," laughed Stella, astride their path, less an Amazon than a rosy-fingered Dawn. Angus crouched at her side.

"But a small army was chasing you!" cried Nod.

"Or thought they were. Now they're chasing each other in a forest of wheat and a tangle of grapevines sharp with broken trellises."

"You magicked them?"

"You could call it that. In the misty light of the dawn, a running figure is hard to identify. I threw my voice about, you see, and Angus helped me confuse them, and—"

"Like a circus showman!" said Nod, though the light was surprisingly clear. "And Tutelina fought like Minerva—and looked like Venus!"

"And Nod has proved to be my quickest pupil," said Tutelina, pride ashine in her eyes between the blinks.

"Did I?" asked Nod. "If we just had time—"

"Time is another name for Proteus," Stella reminded. "Beware of his shifting shapes."

"Nod," whispered Dylan. "See them bodies on the ground?"

"Revellers, I expect. Still unconscious from wine or blows."

"Wearin' robes? Christians, lad! The ones who give chase. Stella's *eldritch*."

"And now for the cave," said Stella, smiling her sweet compulsion.

And so they made for Cedalion's hideaway, and Dylan's boat, and—who could say?—pursuing Christians and hungry demons with a taste for boys.

And so they began the journey of their lives (or was it *for* their lives?).

Part II:
JOURNIES

★ Chapter One ★

"Untidy," sighed Dylan, extending his hand to include the whole of his cave, his borrowed tomb, his makeshift, rock-walled home. He could not have characterized the place with a more—to him—disagreeable adjective. Untidy. Unlovable. Unlivable.

"Tidy," said Stella with mild reproach. "Burial vaults aren't exactly villas, whatever the old Etruscans liked to pretend. They're indoors and outdoors at the same time." Indoors or outdoors, her beauty metamorphosed but did not diminish: then, a sunburst, now a soft suffusion which tempted the hand to stroke or the head to nest.

"Truly?" asked Dylan, brightening as if he had speared a succulent mackerel.

"You have dusted the murals till every banqueter seems about to—" The banqueters, scantily clad, men and women embracing on slender couches, slave girls naked except for gilded sandals, slave boys naked without exception and clearly meant for dessert, seemed more inclined to copulate than eat, in spite of the delicacies spread before them: dormouse in tunny sauce, flowering elecampane, thrush on asparagus. "About to take his pleasure." A safe, general term. Stella was hardly a prude, but she seemed to respect Dylan's lateness in coming to love. "Your clothes chest is fragrant with cedar. Your pans are old but free of rust. Your patera is clean as well as beautifully wrought." Dylan's patera, his own creation and not a gift from the builders of the tomb, was a copper cup, whose handle resembled a Siren girl. "Your haricot beans are fresh—"

"Picked 'em before the festival. Have to dry 'em for Angus, though."

"And there is no smell of fish," said Tutelina, eying

Dylan's gills but hastening to add, "Not that there should be. Tritons don't smell fishy either."

"You ought to know," said Stella, vexed with her tactless friend. "I believe you have had a number of them for lovers."

"Only six. Or was it seven? All in all, they're much inferior to Roanes, or so I should think. Too much tail."

"Scaly too," said Dylan, who had no affection for Tritons, a race which divided its time between gorging food, chasing Sirens, and picking fights with inoffensive dolphins.

"I think," said Nod, "that we ought to see to the boat." In the roseate light of the brazier, he looked unaccountably pale. He patted the image of Lordon which hung from his neck; the little bronze image was good for luck in general as well as love.

Of course! thought Dylan. *Goin' to leave his mother.* Mothers in general were unfamiliar to Dylan, and hitherto unappealing and even harsh. *They deserted bairns on desolate beaches.* But Nod had been *found* by a mother.

"This way, Nod, Stella, Tutelina," said Dylan, relishing the sound of their names, their newfound friendship, their reliance on him, a lowly Roane. "Angus, bring up the rear." He lit a lamp from the brazier and moved his chest to reveal a circular ladder cut into walls of rock.

He took Stella's arm to guide her steps. "Rough goin'," he said. (In truth, the descent was smooth; after the festival, why did he need an excuse for a minor intimacy? Perhaps because she had threatened to leave him for another lover. (*Would have too. 'Cept for the Christians.*)

She was warm and soft, and fragrant with honeysuckle, and her loosened hair, ignoring its fillet, brushed his naked shoulders and sent a flame from his murex-ears to his webbed toes. For once, he did not regret the lack of a seal skin to hide his nakedness. Stella had freed him from shame.

"Dearest Dylan," she said, encircling him with her arm. "It is you who will rescue us from this cold, Christian land. Do you know your power?"

"Power, ma'am?" To fight, to swim, to row? His arms

were powerful, his thighs were supple and strong. But
these were the birthright of many men and Roanes. She
seemed to imply a rarer girl—to divine the future in the
entrails of a sheep; to change his shape like Proteus, god
of the sea; to—But Stella's pronouncements would have
confounded a Sibyl.

"Never mind. This isn't the time. Let it be enough that
we trust and follow you. That I—I—" She stammered
into silence and shyly withdrew her arm. Without hesita-
tion, he returned it to his shoulder. Was he presumptu-
ous? No, she held him so tightly that he almost dropped
the lamp; she a corn Sprite; he a humble Roane!

The smell of man and his varied possessions yielded to
the faint acidity of volcanic tufa. They had left the world
of men. They had entered the world of demons. He heard
the rustling of the underground river, a serpent dragging
its length through dry, brown stones. He stepped from the
last rung and gathered his friends about him and saw the
reddish water dip and disappear into a recess like the
mouth of a ravenous Cylcops.

Then they came to the ship. . . .

Boat, actually, or something between the two, small but
not too small to wrestle the sea. For Dylan, like every
good sailor, knew that five-tiered quinqueremes had
floundered in waters safely navigated by fishing boats.
The captain and sailors made the difference; they and
their guardian gods. (Had not the goddess Leucothea,
she of the ivory hands, rescued Ulysses from drowning
and sent him to hospitable shores?)

The ship (the boat) held a tall, single mast with lowered sail, and a rounded wicker cabin resembling a beehive, whose hatch was flanked by images of Bonus Eventus and a matching Lordon carved to Nod's direction. She
was one of those arc-shaped boats, her hull of twisted papyrus stalks, which the ancient Egyptians had built before
the founding of Rome, before the Etruscans had come to
Italia, before the fall of Troy. Papyrus grew in a swamp
to the south of Misna. The other materials Dylan had
found in the tomb.

Her name was the *Stella*.

"Will it carry us to Britannia?" asked Nod. "The Egyptians never mastered the Great Green Sea, and Oceanus filled them with terror. Or so my pedagogue said."

"Bonus Eventus willin'. Egyptians hadn't no keels to their ships. Struck a shoal and burst like a blowfish. This un's got a keel."

"How did you know how to build her? She isn't like the coracle you told me about." Nod no longer looked pale; his face was flushed with pride and his smile would have warmed the heart of Medusa, the Gorgon whose stare could turn a man into stone. (*Proud o' me, that boy. 'Cause I built a ship. 'Cause I'm his friend.*)

"Remembered," he said. Where, when, how? Such matters escaped him. The past had opened a hatch; he had peered through the misty opening, spied a vessel, and copied her for his escape. The mists had gathered and darkened, the hatch had closed and battened against his scrutiny.

A small rope ladder hung from the deck. Dylan began his ascent and lowered an arm to Stella—not that she needed help, but she took the arm with an admirable balance of femininity and force. Nod gave a hand to Tutelina. Blinking, she flailed the air like a woman assaulted by hornets, but caught his fingers and captured them in an inextricable clasp. And finally all of them stood on the deck, the mast awaiting a sail as a Christian awaits a robe, the hatch to the cabin offering an invitation. Angus crouched at the foot of the ladder, ready to loosen the mooring lines at a sign from his master. With six legs, he appeared to be born for the task.

"The ladies can rest in the cabin," said Dylan. "Sailorin's a man's job." He opened the hatch but quickly withdrew his head. *"Already somethin' in there."*

"That isn't something, that's my mother," said Nod, peering over Dylan's shoulder.

Draped in voluminous robes, she rose from a three-legged stool to engulf her son in a hearty maternal embrace.

"Nod, Nod, could you have left your mother without goodbye?"

He surpassed her hug. "We couldn't risk a return to the town. Father is after us."

"I know. I wanted to warn you but he never let me out of his sight till he led his friends to the fields. I call him Argus-eyed, you know. Behind his back."

"I know what you mean," smiled Nod. "Eyes of Argus, temper of Polyphemus, the old Cyclops."

"How'd you find the ship?" asked Dylan. Not even the demoness, so he had thought, had known of this cave, plans for flight, the underground river shown to him by the Siren girl and leading to the sea.

"I've been exploring these caves for years," she said. "My husband's key, don't you know. I slipped it out of his pouch a hundred times! Not that I care for the wine; it's very cheap. I wondered, though, what he did in his cave." A woman of middle years, she made a wonder of graying hair and wrinkled hands. She smelled at once of kitchens and gardens, and you thought of the sun on morning glories, or the marvel of new-baked bread. She was a beautiful woman in whom no single feature was smooth or young. Beauty stared from her eyes and illuminated her face like the haloes imagined by the legions of Christ. *Nod's adoptive mother? Wonder if she'd adopt a Roane.*

"But there's a demoness about."

"Yes, I met her the first day. But I know the proper spell to keep her at bay. I have some Etruscan blood, you see."

"I didn't know that, Mother. You can protect us then, and we can protect you. You will just have to join us on our voyage. We can't leave you with *him*."

"I've been with him for something like twenty years," she said, between a smile and a sigh. "It has been an adventure."

"But he tried to crucify Tutelina!"

"Yes," said Tutelina, blinking and breathless. "And he turned me upside down. And all those lecherous men—how they ogled me."

"The possible crucifixion arouses my deepest sympathy, though it does not surprise me," said Marcia. "As for the

ogling, well, at times I regret that I became a Christian,
That is to say, when I still deserved an ogle."

"Mother," cried Nod. "Aren't you ashamed. You're
much too—too—"

"Old for such talk? Possibly. For wishing, no. In
twenty years, your father has given me a single gift. A
hood to wear in the basilica. Used at that. If my thoughts
have strayed, well, it was because my spirit cavorted with
the ancients."

"You never talked this way before. You sound like
me!"

"*He* was always about. Besides, I am going to lose my
son. At such a time it is very hard to be a stoical Christian lady." She did not attempt to hide her tears.

What's the shame? thought Dylan. *Shows what she
feels. Love her for it.*

"What is hello without goodbye?" asked Stella, hushed
till now, hushed like a sail without any wind. "Dearest
Marcia. I think—I know—you will see your son again."
The women exchanged a look which was hard to read.

"Soon?"

"Soon."

A radiant woman, Marcia. The kind of a woman to
have for a mother (unless one wished to be forsaken in
Caledonia). He hated to see her separated from Nod and
left with that despoiler of festivals, that would-be crucifier
of Sprites, her husband (and hated to lose a chance at
adoption).

"Ship's ready to sail," he announced. "Got to provi-
sion her, though. Fill 'er wi' ballast. Food. Water. Then
off to Britannia."

"The ship is already ballasted," said Marcia. "I learned
a bit of the nautical trade from my husband. She is also
provisioned. By the way, what is her name?"

"The *Stella*."

"The *Stella*. The Star. A fortunate name, I think. Myself, I am anything but a star, but at least I have brought
you rectangular cheeses—easy to pack in a tiny space—
and loaves of wheaten bread and flagons of muscatel. And
Dylan, I have included some haricot beans for your

friend"—she smiled at Angus as if he were one of the crew instead of an outsized ant with a penchant for tools—"and the sail is ready to hoist—I mended a small tear."

"But when did you have the time?"

"It was a long festival. It must have been very—mirthful."

"Oh, yes," said Nod, "and I learned all kinds of mirth."

"Indeed? Tell me, dear. Have I been remiss in my education? There is a difference about you. As if you have just won a laurel crown. Perhaps your little god has brought you luck. What kind of mirth did you learn?"

"Oh, how to grow wheat. *That* sort of thing."

"That sort of thing is useful as well as fun, is it not?"

"Hoist sail," cried Dylan.

"There isn't any wind," said Nod. "Why not use the oars?"

"Wind or not, looks better wi' a sail. Current 'ull carry us."

"Dylan," said Marcia. "Will you look after my son?"

"Not to worry, ma'am. Lad's like my own brother."

Dylan tucked a skin around his shoulders and felt its protective magic throb throughout his being.

Demon-haunted caverns.

Oceanus with his mast-high waves.

Forests where even Romans feared to build their roads.

Seizing the till, he shouted to Angus, "Cast off the moorin' lines and clamber aboard, Mate."

The underground river seized them in its coils.

★ Chapter Two ★

To Dylan, the river was strange but strangely known. Guided by Mara, the Siren girl, he had swum its length from the sea and found his cave and his home in the old Etruscan tomb. During his journey, horrors and wonders had lined the bank, and what he had seen had frightened and awed him less than what he imagined slouched in the shadows and deadly—or friendly—to men since the age of heroes like Ulysses and Aeneas. Memory perched in his mind like a bird of prey; talons and beak to rend (or build a nest?).

Now, a return to the sea. . . .

He looked at his friends and mistook them for gods, not Sprites: the comeliness of them, the courage, the grace and the pride (himself so clumsy and plain—web-foot!). Stella, her tunic a silken green, her sash empurpled with murex dye, her legs unemcumbered as if for the chase, one bare shoulder like that of Diana racing deer (but Stella was kind; Diana had murdered Actaeon for spying her nude). Tutelina, a marvel of pink roundnessess which threatened to overflow the bondage of her robe; losing a bosom and restoring it, casually, to its nest. Nod in a loin cloth with a grasshopper clasp (no longer a boy nor quite a man. Nod who must be protected but made to feel protector).

"Dylan," said Stella, watching him watch her, guessing his deepest thought. "The scars you got in the galley—is that why you wear that flimsy cloak?"

"Wear it for luck. In place o' the seal."

"That's all right then. I was going to say, you've noth-ing to hide. Dylan, my beautiful."

"Mean it, Stella, girl?"

"I have seen many men. Yes, and gods. But you, my dear. . . ."

100

"A garden of love!" cried Nod, pointing to vegetation along the bank as they rounded a sudden curve.

"Sort o' a little Not-World," Dylan mused, remembering what he had heard of a forest in Britannia, a place of eternal love, where the veins embraced the trees, and the rivers flowed with ale, and the fish swam into your nets or took your lines, and, as for the men and women, they had their choice of many or chose the one and never needed to sleep (*good place for Nod and Tutelina. Wouldn't even stop to tipple*).

Here, the flowers were as large as trees. Some, like enormous breasts, mimicked the color of a woman's flesh. Some, like the white hands of courtesans offering love, languished toward the boat, to give, to take. Mandrake stems like enormous phalli hinted at buried roots, man-shaped, which, when dissolved in the milk of a goat assured a woman of children: a larger root for a boy, a smaller root for a girl. Powdered mandrake, mixed in honey cakes, restored potency to impotent men, and awoke desire in frigid virgins. The scent of the place was myrrh and musk, vegetable and animal at once; the murmur was like the voices of lovers, intimately locked in love.

"Dylan," asked Tutelina. "Do you think we might drop anchor and, uh, dally among the flowers? Nod and I—perhaps we can bring them a touch of the sun and enjoy an *interlude*."

"Stella and me too," announced Dylan. *Think I'm a bloody monk, do they? Learnt my lessons well as Nod. Just don't prattle so much.*

"It's far too sad a place to linger," said Stella. "You rarely see these plants above the ground. The Christians uproot them as signs of their evil demon, Satan. And yet they speak of love and all that is natural between a man and a woman. Here, such a garden can never thrive, though planted by loving hands."

"My mother has always said that Christ is love, though his followers sometimes forget the fact."

"True. He loved the Magdalene, and she was a desert Sprite, lost in the city and pining for her red rocks and

black poppies, and fennecs, like little foxes with outsized
ears. But there was Paul to distort his truths. Paul was a
vengeful man. A woman scorned him once. . . . He never
forgot."

Behind them, the garden flickered into unnatural dusk,
the outstretched hands fell languidly, emptily toward the
water . . . the murmur resembled the wail of spirits lack-
ing a coin to cross the Styx. Then there were barren rocks
of volcanic tufa and scorched, blackened walls, and the
stench of sulphur and slime. . . . And footprints to fit a
giant.

"I expect to see Dis with every twist of the river," said
Tutelina. "The burning eyes, the bristling beard. . . ."

"He is no one to fear."

"But Stella, he ravished Proserpine."

"And gave her a throne, and loved her as a bride. He,
the lonely. King of an Underworld without a queen. He
spied her, still a virgin, wreathing garlands along the
slopes of Aetna. What should he do but steal her to sit at
his side and help him to render justice to his subjects, the
shades of kings and slaves? And half of every year he suf-
fered her to return to the surface and rejoin her mother,
Ceres." Stella shrugged and quickly ended her tale, like a
mother whose children have gone to sleep (but no one
slept on that ship). "Or so the story goes. It was ages
ago. . . . Now he has fled, no doubt, before the advance of
the Desert King. Perhap she is dead."

"Dead?" cried Dylan. "But gods are immortal."

"Only so long as they are worshipped and needed. The
people offer them sacrifices of burnt meat and new wine.
But it is worship they eat and need they drink. It is the
Christians whom we have to fear. Or demons older than
Dis. . . ." Her voice became a wisp. She, the enigma, she,
the unfearing, seemed lost like a little girl in a forest of
spiders and bats.

"There, there, lass," Dylan consoled, folding the
sotfness of her, strangely chill, into his arms and drawing
his cloak around the both of them. "Got a ship to protect
us. A stout crew. And Angus here who's worth a' army
what wi' those feelers o' his."

"You don't understand the dangers," she said. "You're only a boy."

"Sixteen! Older than Nod here. Journeyed more than Ulysses. Seen giants like walkin' towers and pygmies on the backs o' cranes. Toiled and fought and—"

"There are dangers worse than giants."

"Been here before!" he asked, surprised. Fertility Sprites, or so he supposed, kept to the surface, with its grain and its olive trees and its plenitude of sun. Except for the garden of Venus, this was a world for barren rocks and demons without a heart.

"Yes." She looked as if she had seen Medusa's head. A whispered "when?" would have turned her into stone.

"Is that a forest?" asked Nod. "Trees along the bank." Then, with incredulity. "Cypress without any sun?"

"Lichens," said Dylan. "Big as trees down here."

Their mottled branches, orange and black and brown in one great tumult of leaf and limb, held no hint of green, remembrance of surface or sun.

Tutelina sighed and crossed her arms above her breasts. There was something at once courageous and wistful about the move, a Corn Sprite, fecund and lushly beautiful, protecting the emblem of her fecundity in a barren land. "They're twisted and torn, like a woman's hair when she has clawed it in grief. Forsaken in love."

Stella trembled in Dylan's embrace. Strange, he loved the loveliness of her, the courage, the mystery. Best, he loved her tremulous in his arms.

Some of the lichens trailed their vegetable tresses in the water, as if they lacked the strength or the will to stand; as if a sorrow had bent them like grieving women; they reeked of ashes and burnt olive oil, the scent of mourning instead of morning. The light from the cavern filtered among their branches, showing the colors, bleached or muted; figuring shapes which to Dylan's fancy were almost human; women yes, and sad; or furious Bacchae finding a man at a woman's festival.

"That tree has nipples on its trunk," cried Nod. "And the growth at its foot—it seems to be babies all tumbled together. And—and—they seem to be moving!"

"Are movin'. Sometimes one breaks loose in the river and drowns. Or floats apiece and sprouts a new Zieba tree. Saw some on my way up. Not babies, though. Fruit, that's all. Don't pine for 'em, lad."

"Is it far to the sea?" asked Tutelina, holding to Nod as if she were vampirizing him (though he a happy victim). "I would give a hundred years of my life for a sight of the sun!"

"Swimmin' upstream took, oh, 'bout four days. Down oughta be quicker." Dylan reflected upon his crew, totally inexperienced except for himself (or thus he supposed; thus he knew about Nod. But Stella. What was beyond her knowledge? He had seen her unshaken against a mob with staves. Now she was marble; unapproachable; hidden within a secret, the sacred image in the holy of holies. He did not even dare to touch her hand. Lightning would strike him or he would turn to dust.

And yet, foolishly perhaps, he did not doubt that he could lead them to the sea. Had anyone ever been blessed with such remarkable friends, and one of them—when she chose—his own particular lass (in spite of her having other lads)?

"Let's have some cheer," he forced himself to say. "Stella, give us a song."

"It isn't a time for songs."

"For love?" asked Nod, looking hopefully at Tutelina.

"I think Nod has made an *excellent* suggestion. Two of us could man the ship, while the other two, well, enjoyed an *interlude*. Ceres knows, we need a respite. I feel quite wasted with fear."

"Don't you understand? We have begun our final journey." Her face was blanched of color, a poppy bereft of the sun.

"A song help's the voyagin'," persisted Dylan. "Sailors sing when they row to battle. Nod, my lad. Something—"

"Bawdy?"

"Goin' to say bonny."

"Don't be a prude, Dylan. You're a sailor, aren't you? Sailor songs have to be bawdy. All the time they're at sea,

sailors think about the women waiting for them on the
shore. Isn't that right?"

"Nay, lad, mostly they think about liftin' them bloody
oars out o' the water, droppin' canvas, and bidin'."

"In the arms of a beautiful woman."

"In the arms o' Morpheus, as the poet says."

How could they speak so lightly at such a time? Dylan
looked to Stella for understanding. Words were better
than windless silence, serpent-slithering water, the squish
of the prow against a piece of wood, a root, a flower in
the shape of a human head. . . .

"Ugh," said Nod. "That looked like a baby we hit."

"Got no feelin'. Fruit of the Zieba tree."

The creature, red and wrinkled like an aborted child,
quivered out of the way. Perhaps it would light on the
shore and sprout another tree, another mother to many
abortions.

*Mother. Great Mother. Ceres. Underworld's a place
wi'out any Mother. Even the King quit his throne. Who
wants to rule a country like this?*

Motherless, kingless, friendless, except for the *Stella*
valiantly struggling toward the sea.

The river looped abruptly, a serpent changing its mind.
The vessel struck the bank and squished to a halt. No
trees here, neither garden of love nor funereal lichens.
And the cavern roof seemed to hoard its light, glistening
like a huge, pale cerement about to fall on the ship;
scarcely illuminating the river, the deck, and the mariners;
leaving the bank in shadows and deeper darknesses.
Beside them an ancient ferry, its prow concealed by earth
and lichens, its stern thrust into the river, disintegrating
under the flow of the water. On a raised cypress platform
at the prow, some forgotten ferryman—Etruscan? De-
monic?—had stood and poled his friends or his prisoners,
to freedom or prison.

"Has something grabbed us?" asked Tutelina. "Are we
going to be ravished?"

"Stuck, that's all. "Ull give us a nudge wi' the polin'
oar." *Ugh. Lichens look like spiders. No more women,
pinin' or not.*

He felt and heard the snap of the oar before he saw the shadowy being who had snapped it between its jaws, or felt the jaws envelop his head.

He thought at first that his head had been severed from his body. His body lost sensation; only his head could feel, hear, smell: a clammy fur, a constriction which was almost a crushing, a stench like rotting roots in a Celtic tarn.

No, his limp body dangled from his encompassed head; wrenched but not decapitated, he had been jerked from the deck, snapped like a cat-o-nine with the suddenness of the movement, and dropped in a nest of lichenous under-growth. He spat a bitter liquid out of his mouth and gulped breaths to prepare for another assault. Two yellow eyes appraised and condemned him; an open mouth por-tended an imminent feast. Four yellow eyes ... six ... eight. . . .

Cerberus, the six-headed dog which had guarded the Underworld in the ancient time. A myth ... at most, a memory . . . now, a confrontation.

Well, if he could talk to a six-legged ant, why not a six-headed dog? Sweet-talk, it seemed, must arrest the de-scending maw. *Nod, had I your eloquence, lad. . . .*

"There, old fellow. Dinna mean you harm—"

The head paused, swayed, exulted above its prey. In the dim light, he saw the fur and the teeth and, always, the yellow eyes.

He opened his mouth to call to his friends. Even a weathered sailor could use some help. "Ahoy there!"

But his friends had another concern.

"Genita Mana!" It was Stella's voice; surprise, strengthening into resolution.

"The old cow," cried Nod. "We should have guessed she would track us."

"Well, at least she isn't a Christian," said Tutelina. "Though she's skinny enough for a martyr, isn't she?"

And what about him, Dylan, crouching ignominiously among the lichens? And nobody seemed to have noticed his loss, or noticed Cerberus, barring him from the ship!

"We don't know my mothers' spells," said Nod. "How

shall we ward her off? Dylan, what do you—Dylan, where are you?"

"Dylan!" Stella's cry was like a sword in his hand.

"Ain't an old cow after *me*," said Dylan. "Old dog, that's what. Never mind. Seen worse in my day. Scylla, for instance. Talk about heads—" A head swung like a Persian executioner's ax and swatted him into silence. Apparently Cerberus brooked no rival.

He heard a frantic scrambling aboard the ship, a confusion of voices. Nod. Tutelina. Stella. "Something's got Dylan." "What is it?" "Looks like an octopus. No, a dog." "Cerberus!" "Grab another oar and smite its neck ... necks."

But darkness and distance made his rescue a feat if not an impossibility. He must become his own champion. Stella could handle a demon—he hoped—with conjurations and evil eyes, but who could harness a six-headed dog?

"Let me go," he boomed at the dog, enveloping all of the heads with his best nautical roar, a kind of vocal net. "*Said* I meant you no harm." But the beast refused to be trapped or cowed.

Genita, kneeling and smiling, began to moor the ship to a lichen stump.

"Did you presume that alone I came to accost four Sprites?" she asked in her curiously polished, archaic Latin. He saw her dimly and wished for a deeper dark. So tall that her head brushed the earthen roof, white as a blowfish belly, her breasts an intimation instead of a presence, she smiled and displayed her rotten teeth. In the shadows behind her crouched the dog. In the shadows under the dog, crouched Dylan, slapped to the ground with another head whenever he tired to rise. Cerberus looked as large as six lions, and each of the heads, no doubt, could boast a proportionate bite.

"A head for each of you counting Angus," smirked Genita, "and one to spare. It shall have half of the portly one."

"Are you calling me fat?" snappped Tutelina. "Whoever heard of a skinny corn Sprite?"

"I think she meant voluptuous," consoled Nod.

The babble of voices subsided into silence. *Nobody*

knows what the Hell to do. 'Fraid to speak. Never mind.
As soon a dog as a shark. Sailor's life's a short 'un, one
way or another. Friends, though. They got to reach the
sea. Maybe I can, as it were, keep 'im busy eatin' while
the boat sails on. Wriggle and break a tooth and stomp a
paw. . . .

"Genita," commanded Stella, daylight commanding the
dark. "Both of us belong to the earth, but I am of the sun."

Genia's laughter resounded among the sunless hillocks
of tufa, the river of blood, the spider-colored lichens.
"Then I suggest you order an immediate sunrise. Or perhaps a high noon."

"I have brought the sun with me." Carefully, as if she
were handling amber and amethysts, Stella withdrew the
pouch from between her breasts and extracted a handful
of crushed, dried petals.

"Flowers? Dead flowers? Don't insult me with such a
charm. Cerberus, you may dispatch the Roane at once.
Then the golden boy. Linger on him. Savor him morsel by
morsel. Next, the women. One will give you a feast."

"Cerberus!" It was Stella's cry. "Release my friend."
Then she flung the petals into Genita's face.

The scent of dried narcissi pervaded the air; aromatic
to men; anathema to demons.

Genita dropped her line and covered her eyes as if the
petals were sparks from a guttering brazier. The roar she
uttered was that of a man, or so it sounded to Dylan's
sensitive ears. Not that he was surprised. *Always looked*
like a man, 'cept for those nubs o' breast and what she
hadn't below.

He searched for the nubs of breast—in vain. And what
she had below was unexceptional but undeniable.

Genita Mana had been replaced by Marcus; the
bleached, inhumanly tall woman by a white, naked man,
cowering into the undergrowth to hide his nakedness.
Cerberus seemed befuddled by his mistress' loss. His
heads swung indecisively between his prisoner and the
naked man; searched the lichens, scanned the wrinkled
roof. *Stupid hound. Can't think for hisself.*

"Stella," cried Nod. "Throw some more petals. Get the

dog before he gets Dylan. The man's no threat. He's afraid of us."

"We must find another way. Cerberus isn't a demon."

"But where's Genita?" asked Tutelina. "That old man is the very one who ogled me."

"Father!" cried Nod. "I might have guessed. Your friends with that hideous demon who tried to eat me. That's why you visit the caves."

"Friends?" snapped Tutelina. "I expect they couch together."

Snatching leaves to cover his private parts (Christian in *that* at least), Marcus regained his composure; rising, he smiled his slow and arrogant smile. His face resembled a leathern shield, scarred with the blows of ax and sword; strong, however. Wrought for survival and vengeance.

"Nod, my boy. You refused to become a Christian. Stole my key and invaded my catacombs. Ran away from me. Went to a heathen orgy. I have followed your boat from the start, and now you shall feed my beast. And Stella, I need not say why you shall complete his meal."

Stella's face looked old with remembering. A bronze which has lain in the earth uncountable centuries. "Whatever you call yourself, you are the foe of love. I punished you once. I—"

"Enough," he snapped.

"I punished you because—"

"Enough! I did not ask you to recount my shame."

Stella caught him implacably in her stare. He did not move. His smile was the player's mask in a comedy, but hatred stared through the eyes. "That time when you and your friends tried to crucify Tutelina, I followed you into the fields and caught you in my stare, even as now."

"The evil eye?" asked Dylan.

"Transfixed you to the spot. Then, with your own knife—"

He wrenched himself from the stare. "You turned me into a monk, you infernal woman."

"Infernal? Then we are equally matched."

"Stella, what does my father mean?"

"I made him a eunuch, like a priest of Cybele."

"Stella, how clever of you!" said Tutelina. "That wretched man will never upend and ogle me again. Even if he does, all he can do is look. But no one has told me where you hid Genita."

"Why, nowhere. She—he—hasn't taken a step. It is often true of Etruscan demons that they can assume a human shape and even alter their sex. Genita, the queen of demons, became a man at will. Until I burned her with petals and forced the change. At least for the moment."

"Eldritch," whispered Dylan.

"It is nothing of the kind. A Lamia changes shape. Woman by day, blood-sucking bat by night. And you, Dylan, doubtless know of Proteus, the sea-god, who can become a fish or a bird or a shark."

"But how can a demon become a Christian?" demanded Nod.

"The Christians destroy demons like me," shrugged Marcus. "If they catch us. What better place to hide than in their midst? And theirs is the coming faith. Who can say, I may become a bishop? Since Stella has narrowed my other choices."

"Think of it this way," Tutelina observed. "You will have no distractions."

Nod: "But what about my mother? Surely she knows what you are."

"Marcia? Poor, foolish woman, she dotes upon me. Believes all that nonsense of turning the other cheek."

"You won't harm her?"

"Oh, I may beat her when she is more than usually stupid. Beatings are good for women. Keeps them in the house and out of sin. Otherwise, why should I harm her? She is the perfect disguise. Who could suspect the husband of such an exemplary woman?"

"And the Desert King? Won't he smite you in his wrath? After all, a *demon*. Christ was always driving them out of herds and such."

"That was Christ. This is the Desert King. I rather expect he likes me better than those namby-pamby Christians who turn the other cheek. He has always been one for sending plagues and leveling cities."

"I want to go back," said Nod. "I can't leave my mother with such a creature."

"You can't go back, my dear," said Stella. "We have begun the ultimate journey. It must be completed, whatever awaits us. Trust me. Your mother will not be harmed."

"You have not seen the last of me," said Marcus. An ancient scar, won in a war with the Gauls, shone scarletly down his cheek. It seemed to burn with the fires of his own unextinguishable anger.

"Or you of us," said Stalla. "Loosen the line."

"I shall follow you to the sea and across the sea! And never again shall you catch me with your stare."

"Loosen the bloody line," barked Dylan. Cerberus, who had recovered his poise (pose? He spread his heads like so many poppy petals, as if to be admired), awaited orders from his mistress-become-a-master. Furtively, Dylan attempted to rise; a crouch became a stand. Six heads glowered him to his knees; then, writhed away from him in surprise and alarm.

Angus had scuttled to his master's defense. The six-legged Telchin confronted the giant with clacking jaws and feelers wielded like swords. . . . The giant confronted the Telchin with six quizzical faces. So paltry a foe, they seemed to say. And yet, and yet. . . . A single head can have a pair of jaws, and jaws may bite, and the bite be as poisonous as a viper's sting. Angus began to circle the giant; the heads followed him until they became entangled and started to bark. The body concealed in the shadows, shapeless, canine or not it was hard to say, remained surprisingly rooted to the spot.

Of course! Cerberus was a plant, a gigantic Dog Rose from the Golden Age, benign in his day but doubtless soured with the times, or trained in mischief by one of his chthonian masters. Only his heads could move. The "fur" was foliage.

Then, the incredible. No, the predictable. After all, Angus and Cerberus both had an inclination for sixes.

Their mutual circling slowed to a stately dance. They

stared, assessed, concluded. Angus extended a tentative
feeler and stroked a head, two, three—

Cerberus uttered a moan of satisfaction, like that of a
petted dog (actually, a chorus of moans).

Friends!

Dylan sprang to his feet and clambered through lichens—Proteus, how they prickled his webbed feet!—
down the bank and, seizing Nod's hand, up the side of his
ship. Cerberus hardly appeared to notice his absence. Nod
and Stella and Tutelina more than noticed his presence;
they crowded to hug him, Stella kissing his cheek, Nod
squeezing his ear. He was home; he was loved; he could
fight an underworld of dogs or demons!

The Captain resumed command. "Angus, time to lift
sail!"

Reluctantly Angus clambored aboard the ship. Cerberus
leaned his heads toward his new-found friend, in supplica-
tion, not anger. "Stay, stay, stay," they seemed to plead.

"Loosen the bloody line," cried Dylan to Marcus.
"Cerberus ain't your minion anymore. Eat you if I say the
word. Fellow's hungry, that's clear enough. And Angus
bites like a barracuda."

Marcus dropped his concealment of leaves as he bent
to unmoor the ship. He rose, revealed in his nakedness,
the white, weathered skin, the wounds from foreign wars
and Stella's knife. But it was shame, not age, which made
him hideous. An ancient Centaur, gnarled as an oaken
trunk, would not have been ashamed of his body, and he
would have been as beautiful as the tree.

On the second day of their journey, the Styx flowed
sluggishly into the sea, as if she wished to reserve her
muddy waters; the *Stella*, afloat the mud, emerged like an
albatross from its secret nest.

"That was only a trial," said Dylan, the doughty mariner. "Now for the *voyage*."

Then they discovered another passenger: tenderly held
in Angus' mouth, a seed as large as a pear, an offspring of
Cerberus throbbing with inner life.

He had been she.

★ Chapter Three ★

"Blue sea, green sea, amethystine sea. . . ."

Nod had woven a song about their journey, which made him think of the Argonauts, in quest of the Golden Fleece.

"Do you know," he said, "I think I'm getting quite tipsy just from all those colors."

"Sea-sick, more likely," said Dylan.

"Sea-*well*. Except for the garden of love, the cave was a dreadful place. I felt as if we had lost the sun forever."

"Only there two days," reminded Dylan, inordinately pleased by the speed of his little craft."

"And now we have weeks of safety and sunshine."

"And a chance for Cerberus' seed to grow in his pot." (Argus had planted the seed in some dirt he had scooped from the river bank at the mouth of the Sytx.)

"And interludes," added Tutelina, encompassing Nod as comfortably as a familiar cloak. "Blue sea, green sea, amethyst, and *me*."

Only Stella was silent and restless; sad, one might almost say. In conversation she could be cheerful and even merry, blessing whatever gods had insured their escape, asking Dylan about the moods of the sea and the coasts of Caledonia. Alone, she sat at the stern, hushed as a masthead, and stared at the dwindling, then invisible mass of Italia.

"Homesick, lass?" asked Dylan, forgetting to man the till.

Quickly she smiled and climbed the platform to stand at his side. "You are my home. Why should I pine for a country where my friends are dead or in hiding? Only a fool looks back. . . ."

Stella was not a fool. Why did she whisper a—blessing?—an incantation?—a cry to the past?

They did not hug the coast in the manner of Roman ships (the foes of Roma called her the sea-fearing, not the sea-faring); they had no time. They skirted islands and sealanes, kept out of sight from shore, and, helped by the wind, a gentle ally, aimed for the Pillars of Hercules. Dylan's instinct was better than any bearing of stars.

"Roane never forgets where he's been. And old Marcus can't catch us even in his trireme. Cause he'll follow the coast. Italia. Hispania. Weeks out o' the way."

"Are you sure?" asked Nod. "He seemed awfully angry at losing his wherewithal. He might anticipate our plan. His ship is a giant shark, my mother says. Grappling hooks and battering ram, three sails and sixty oars. If he follows our route, he can overtake and sink us."

"Stella put the fear o' Neptune in him. He'll follow the coast if he follows at all."

"Very well," said Nod. "Let's enjoy the voyage. Tutelina, what were you saying?"

"An int—"

"Exactly."

They fled to the cabin and battened the hatch. It was a place for love: small, intimate, shadowy; fragrant with salt-breezes and cedar chests. The close-meshed hammock embraced their own embrace. "Do you know," said Nod, "that except for you I am still a virgin?"

"You would have lain with Stella at the festival." She smelled of the myrrh which she wore in a tiny vial between her breasts. In the dim cabin, she seemed more fragrance than presence.

"That was then. That was Lordon's doing. Now she is like a sister to me."

"Would you call me a sufficiency then, my dear?"

"An abundance. A harvest home."

"*Please.* You make me sound fat."

"I meant *voluptuous.*"

"Faithful Nod! Lord of my hills and valleys."

"But Dylan and Stella, I think, are neglecting their interludes."

"Stella, you see, remembers."

"What, exactly?"

"Before I knew her she was—loved. She can't forget."

"Well, we must enjoy ourselves for both of them."

Day followed day with no ship in sight; luck followed luck and brought them a rare white dolphin to frolic in their wake.

"Delphus," Dylan explained. "Kind o' a fishy god. Met him before. Know him by his gold. Look, he's brought us a gift!"

Delphus lifted a conch shell full of clams. Then, his gift received, he sat on his tail, awaiting approval and gratitude. For dolphins, however generous, liked to be thanked.

"If he's a godling, a gift isn't enough," said Nod. "We must make him an offering. Do you think he would like a libation of wine?"

"Bread," said Dylan. "Hard to get down there. Goes well wi' fish."

They took a loaf of bread from the wicker basket woven by Marcus' mother, a princely gift from such a diminutive larder, and joined hands while Stella spoke a prayer:

"From the land to the sea, a gift. Bread wrought of wheat and blessed by the spirits of earth."

"And a Roane."

"And a Roane. For one of the kings of the sea."

Then he was gone.

"To share it wi' his friends," said Dylan. "Lovin' folk, those dolphins. Back to work now. Everybody. No more malingerin'. Got to swab the deck."

But Nod and Tutelina, none too eager to scour the decks, escaped to the prow and after a time—long or short, how could a lover judge?—saw a curious sight.

Beside the ship, a head broke the surface and a young girl, pale, serious, silver of hair, stared at the lovers with a disappointment which approached dislike.

"Little girl," called Nod, for he was a youth and she, his junior by several years, a mere child to him. "Do you want to come aboard?"

"I am not a little girl," she snapped. "I am a young

lady, and I have eaten brash young men like you in a single meal. Where is the master of your vessel?"

"Tilling or scouring."

"Oh, well, I mustn't disturb him at his post. For he may have enemies on his trail. Warn him though." With a backward glance at Nod, she went the way of the dolphin.

"A child out here?" asked Nod. "Why, there isn't a coast in sight. Did she fall overboard in a storm?"

"A Siren girl. Delphus must have sent her in search of Dylan. She may be the one who showed him the mouth of the Styx."

"*Here,*" said Dylan, thrusting a long-handled brush at Nod and Tutelina. "*Said* it was time to swab."

"But Dylan, we just saw a—"

"Always moonin' about, you two. Time you learn to work like sailors."

"But we saw a—"

"Sea plays tricks on the eye. SWAB."

Nod was tempted to snap: "Nobody just sixteen is going to order me!" But Dylan was probably missing his interludes with Stella; thus, no doubt, his pique.

It was summer, and not the season for storms. The sea was known as "halcyon" because of the bird which built her nest on its calm and laid her piebald eggs.

Nod had learned to swab.

Tutelina had learned to cook: eggs, oysters, fish. . . .

Dylan had lost his pallor and turned as brown as his friends and forgotten to wear his cloak.

Cerberus' seed had sprouted in Angus' pot, and even a father could not have been so proud.

"Dylan," asked Nod, leaning on his brush. "Do you think we'll really get to Britannia? It seems—well, things have been *too* smooth."

"We'll get there all right. Got the right ship." Almost every part of the *Stella* had come from a forest or marsh: papyrus for the deck; oak for the mast, reeds for the roof of the cabin; elm for the oars and rudder. . . . She was less a ship than a miniature forest venturing, and so far welcomed, away from home and across an alien sea. She did not seem to need a protective god, not Bonus Eventus nor Lordon, whose twin images, resembling brothers, flanked the cabin door. The mariners were the luck of the ship, not the gods; Stella, Tutelina, and Nod, earth Sprites, with a sea Sprite to lead them on their liquid path.

But luck is an hour glass. Sooner or later the glass must be reversed and the sands run ill instead of sweet.

Approaching the Straits, they clove to the northern and Spanish pillar of Hercules. The earth-born son of Jove in one of his celebrated labors had followed a similar route and given his name to the Pillars when he invaded Oceanus and its islands to battle a two-headed dog and steal the red cattle of the giant, Geryones.

But Hercules had been a demi-god raised on his death to Olympus. What did humble Sprites, inclined to love instead of war, and one of them (Nod), a mere provincial youth, know about battling monsters or monstrous seas?

"Straits look calm," said Dylan. "Usually rougher than this."

"Bonus Eventus is smoothing the way," said Nod.

"Land god, that 'un. Sea gods—they got us now. Marcus'ul never catch us, though, if we pass the Straits. Oceanus can be one big Charybdis, but nobody, not all the ships o' Rome, can find us there."

"Dylan," said Nod, peering hesitantly over the stern. "Behind us. Something black. A shark's fin perhaps?"

"Wish it were," said Dylan. He sounded as if he had seen a school of Shellycoats.

"Worse? Honestly, all I see is a little black triangle."

"Trireme. Triple banks o' oars."

"How can you tell at such a distance?"

"Keen eyes."

"Maybe their watchman will overlook us."

"Followin' us."

"But you can't possibly know!"

"See Marcus," he said. "Not his features, mind you. But his shape and his meanness. Copied our trick and didn't stick to the land. Overtakin' us fast."

"Dylan." There was a poignance in Stella's voice.

"Stella, lass?"

"You are a Roane with gills. You can escape. The sea is your element. If it should come to a fight—"

"And leave my friends?" he cried. "We'll fight 'em together."

He slapped his foot on the deck. The webbed toes thumped like a Roman boot.

"With what? They'll ram us or board us or grapple us with hooks. My evil eye is of little use against a ship, and narcissus petals only work against demons. They have us, Dylan."

"*Said* I'd get my friends to Britannia."

Yes, thought Nod. The ladies ravished and me a galley slave. But he gripped the hand of his friend and did his best to lie.

"You will, Dylan, you will."

The trireme uncannily resembled a shark. Slanted, lidless eyes were slashed on the prow; black was the color of hull and railings; the mainsail seemed an enormous fin.

"Speed twice o' ours. Sails and oars and a lot o' men."

"What can we do?" gasped Tutelina. "I fear they have rape in mind as well as capture."

"Just don't *help*," muttered Dylan.

"They are landsmen," said Stella with tactful haste. "Though trained to the sea, they are born of the earth. We shall pray to the gods of the earth."

"Pray all you like," said Dylan, seizing the rudder and starting a zigzag course like that of a waterbug. "Maneuverability's our one defense. Nod, grab a' oar if they overtake us. Tutelina, remember what I said."

But sharks make feasts of lesser fish. . . .

Marcus was standing beside the figurehead at the bow. It was hard to say which looked more weathered and cruel, Marcus or the oaken figure of Moses (doubtless after he had caught his people worshiping Golden Calves). He smiled his slow, cruel smile; the scar on his brow was crimson with unspoken rage. His lips formed a name:

"Nod."

Another: "Stella."

Whoosh, whoosh, whoosh went the great oaken oars, not so much riding the sea as beating her into submission. The rowers, largely concealed behind their protective railings, came into view, impassive, neither pitying not pitiless. Anger and exultation in the chase—these were for free men, these were erased from the faces of galley slaves. They rowed. They rowed because they must.

"Lordon," called Nod. "Be with us now!" For Tutelina, the small defense of his arms he added to prayer.

"He may be dead," whispered Tutelina, "or lost in a faraway land. We have only ourselves to protect ourselves. But you are my shield, and I am not afraid." Once he had underrated her; thought her a simpleton. Once he had been a boy; now he was a man.

It seemed to him scarecely the turn of an hour glass before a gigantic beak—no, a grappling iron—plunged toward their undefended deck.

"Dearest," said Nod. "It's been a happy time."

"The best since the Golden Age!"

"Ain't over yet," snapped Dylan.

The beak fixed on the gunwale and the *Stella* quivered and seemed to die in the water. In vain, the sail puffed with wind. The ship lay idle, caught by the terrible beak. *Edible.* A tunny fish for a shark.

Something rumpled the waters, and not a wind. The sea turned silver, the sea turned green.

The silver and green were heads. Silver-haired and green-haired men. Heads—and hands. And cries which seemed compounded of wind and waves. And laughter, childlike and childishly cruel. And the snapping of many oars. Aboard the trireme, the rowers hunched on their benches, shackled by chains—and apathy. Though a terrible wonder had struck their ship, they did not change expression. They had learned to wait. Forgotten to hope. Come death or freedom, their eyes were dead.

"Idiots," shouted Marcus, not at the slaves—slaves were for rowing—but at his officers, who stood and stared, forgetting the hook, forgetting their spears and bows; men of war who did not remember to fight.

"You've seen Tritons before. Sirens too. *Keep them off the deck.*"

Figures clambered crablike onto the hull, and scuttled over the deck and even up the masts. Sails fell in shreds, the oars were splintered and cast into the sea.

"Nod," said Dylan. "The beak. Help me loosen it from the deck. Sink it."

Stella, strong as a man, joined the men. Tutelina, shouting encouragement, bent her bounteous shoulders with her friends.

Ahead, the Straits. . . . Behind them, a broken and sinking ship.

Hope, like a turquoise halcyon, was their pilot.

Or was it the Siren girl with silver hair?

The ship jarred to a halt; the timbers groaned in the way of papyrus instead of wood, squishes mingled with squeaks; the sail fluttered but not from wind; and the frightened crew, clutching each other's hands, looked to Dylan for answers.

"Run aground?" asked Nod.

"No," said Dylan. "Ain't no ground to run agin here. Ships plied this channel since—since 'fore Stonehenge."

"Stonehenge?"

"The Fingers to the sky. 'Fore the Romans come, folk used to worship there. Or so—"

"Dylan, my dear," said Tutelina. "You may finish your story of Stonehenge another day. I believe that rape is imminent." She pointed a wary finger toward the face which grimaced at them above the railing. "Pirates are boarding the ship, and Stella and I are doubtless the booty."

They had not run aground, they had hit a floating obstruction of floatsam and jetsam, a maze of twisted fibers concealing stones and shells and driftwood, old casks and broken oars and lucky images which had lost their luck. A sea trap built with cunning and hidden under the opaque waters. And one of the trappers had come to confront the trapped.

A Triton.

His hair was the green of seaweed; the fingers which

clutched the gunwale were webbed, and Nod assumed a
greenish tail with translucent scales. In a crude and
graceless way, he was almost attractive, with red, sensual
lips in brilliant contrast to his green hair. But there was
no—caring—in his face. He was the sea, which now
sends sailors on fruitful voyages, now destroys their ships
with maelstroms or waterspouts, the six-headed monster
Scylla or clashing Charybdis.

"Be there only four of you?" cried the Triton. "And all
of you Sprites?"

"Indeed," said Stella. "Fertility Sprites from Italia,
fleeing Christians. We have done you no harm and are not
your enemies."

"I see among you a Roane. The Roanes be not our
friends. And corn Sprites—what be the land to us? What
be its crops?"

"The earth and the sea are sister and brother."

"Families often quarrel. Why do you want to pass into
Oceanus?"

"To find asylum," said Dylan.

"There be no asylum. There be no future." It was
strange to hear a Triton, a child of the moment, speak
with such pessimism. Suddenly he laughed and clambered
onto the deck. "But there be today. Before me I spy two
tasty women with generous flanks."

"Did you hear that, Nod?" whispered Tutelina. "*Generous*. None of your skinny women for him."

"And youths who will please our friends, the Sirens."

"Tutelina," asked Nod. "Have I your permission to
please?"

Dylan poked him and hissed in his ear, "Feastin', that's
their aim. Not love-makin'.' "

Suddenly heads were grinning from starboard and port,
prow and stern. A Siren, shaking the seaweed from her
hair, wriggled onto the deck. No awkward scramble for
her, nor ragged walk. Grace was her manner; hunger
stared from her eyes. The Tritons followed her lead, their
powerful arms propelling them toward the crew, in spite
of their land-sluggish tails; even the tails were able to
thrust and guide.

Dylan raised an oar. Not for his Stella, a slimy Triton's tail!

"There are far too many," she said. "They will ravish Tutelina and me and afterwards drown us. You and Nod shall end at a Siren's feast, and our boat will look like the *Shark*."

"How 'bout your spells? Do what you did to Marcus and the priest."

"They were human. These are Old Ones. Besides, they must be the folk who saved us from Marcus."

"Can't just stand and let 'em take us!"

Tritions love a trade. Sirens too. Give them a gift, and you have made new friends. Temporary, at least."

"How 'bout some bread and cheese?"

"Tutelina," said Stella, ignoring Dylan. "Do you understand what we must do?"

"The Great Mother gave me one skill," smiled Tutelina. "To please men. Tritons, Fauns. Just about everybody"—a disapproving look at Dylan—"except a Roane."

"Don't underestimate yourself," reproved Nod, pressing her shoulder. "Your skills are *uncountable*."

"Thank you, my sweet. If you are right, and if they will help us get through the Straits, I shall be *prodigal*."

"Kind stranger," Stella began to the first invader. "What is your name?"

"Glaucus." He eyed her with admiration and lust. Nod could scent the musk he exhaled from his pores, acrid to men, intoxicating to women. If a man or a Roane, he might have blushed or perspired from the heat of desire. But Tritons, like fish and snakes, were cold-blooded beings, heartless in fact as well as feeling, except for the urge of the flesh. Nod could hardly blame him for his look; thus did he look at his own Tutelina. But to look and to seize were as different as the two faces of Janus. If the Trition should touch her without her consent—well, men had been turned into monks for such an offense.

Her bounty was in her smile. "Glaucus, my friends and I are willing to offer a trade. You can easily take us against our will. Consider, however, before you take. Your tails are designed to splash and frolic and act as weapons against a shark or a Gorgon. In short, to use in the sea. And there they are unsurpasable."

Glaucus beamed assent and appreciation. A Triton's vanity was only surpassed by his lust, and the feature in which he took inordinate pride was his tail, curving robustly from his flanks; colorful too, with scales which resembled thin translucent shells. The fish in him was equal to the man; like Dylan he breathed through gills. Unlike the Roane, his blood was cold.

"But for love-making on the deck of a ship, they are a distinct encumbrance."

"For love-making in the water, they are still an encumbrance," echoed Tutelina, doubtless remembering the disagreeable experience with six—or was it seven?—Tritons.

Glaucus, a tempest in miniature, opened his mouth as if to summon his friends.

"We know such arts," resumed Stella hastily, "my friend and I, to overcome such little awkwardnesses as arise when sea creatures couple with ladies from the land. That is to say, if you invite instead of compel us."

"And what about us?" wailed a Siren, somewhat long in the tooth (she could have bitten an anchor from its chain), her silver hair resembling snow instead of foam, her face as creased as a sand drachma crushed on a beach.

Nod averted his eyes and quickly assumed a Tutelina-blink.

"And *us*," said a younger woman, whose hair held the glitter of sun instead of the frost of age. She flaunted armlets embedded with rainbow shells; she had bound her hair with a fillet of amber beads.

"In spite of my youth, I am not without skill," said Nod. "You could say, in fact, that I'm definitely a tradable commodity." He loved Tutelina, of course (even for conversation). But now was the time to trade.

"Is your eyesight good?" asked the girl.

"Excellent."

"I wasn't sure. The way you blinked. But aren't you a little young?"

"Possibly. But quick to learn."

"Have you the wherewithal?"

"See for yourself. And my friend Dylan is handsome and stalwart and admirably practiced. (Admirably? Tolerably. But friendship required a courteous exaggeration.)

"Won't," snappped Dylan, raising his oar to a deadlier height. "You neither," to Stella.

Stella lifted her arm, which was graced by a single bracelet—black pearls imbedded in gold electrum—and took Dylan's fist and placed it against his side. "You must do as you like, my dear. But all of your friends will die unless we appease these creatures. They are children, these Sirens and Tritons, proud and sometimes cruel. Quick to anger and hurt and even kill. But also easily pleased."

"Canna let 'em have you." But Nod heard weakening in the threat; otherwise, Stella would die.

"Dylan," said Nod in gentle reproof, "do you think that a woman like Stella diminishes herself in the act of giving? Have you ever seen her as less than a goddess? Let her be Venus instead of Minerva to save our lives and ship."

"Yea." Hunched, defeated, he looked like a child who has lost at knucklebones.

Nod took his arm and led him into the cabin, Angus behind them.

"Goin' to lie wi' the Sirens, lad?"

"I'll lie with every Siren aboard this ship! Except," he hurried to add, "the old crone. To get us through the Straits."

Dylan squeezed his arm. "Un'erstand me, lad? About Stella?"

"I understand you, Dylan. And you must understand her."

"Reckon I do. Won't enjoy it, will she?"

"No." (A guess, possibly a lie?)

"And you?"

"Oh, for a time or two, I expect. It seems to be one of my gifts. And Dylan. Don't let Angus out of the cabin. You know what a prude he is."

"Stella, you must sing us a song," cried Tutelina.
And Stella sang:

Halcyon

A halcyon is my love,
Who nested on the sea,
But when I raised a silken net,
My love eluded me.

A halcyon is my love,
Who nested on the sea,
But when I lifted open hands,
My love flew down to me.

"Pretty enough," said Glaucus, "but the songs we sing in our sea-caves are more unbridled."

"Dirty?" asked Nod.

"As a matter of fact," said Tutelina, "I know a few dirty songs myself."

"Tutelina!" cried Nod with mock surprise.

"Have you forgotten our lessons, Nod? Naughty boy!"
And this was her song:

Tailpice

A Triton spied a Siren lass,
And, impudnetly male:
"Observe, my dear, a green carc-*ass*
Which curves into a tail."

"Thank Neptune," said she, "Triton youth
For webbéd hand and scale
And bless him (deity in truth)
For such a *gift* of tail.

A tail so admirably cooth,
So versatile a tail.

As for Nod, he deftly sidestepped the crone—her wizened fingers brushed his loin cloth—and made for the girl who had first caught his eye. To his great surprise, he found that Sirens were novices in the art of love, they were so accustomed to settling for clumsy Tritons, since human males avoided their embraces for fear of becoming dinner instead of lover. Thanks to Tutelina's instruction, he was able to teach the girl some difficult and delightful tricks. He wished of course that she were Tutelina, without any stubby wings or sharpened teeth. But why should he feel a foolish Christian guilt about using his Jove-given tools to save his life and that of his friends? In fact, he enjoyed the girls, the first, the second, the third—it must have been ten at the least. To judge from the fact that they let him muss their hair, they appeared to share in his pleasure and admire his prowess (the first girl returned for a second turn).

Yes, he thought, breathing a prayer to Lordon: "Fertility god and guardian, I am your brother in truth, and what shall a corn Sprite do if not spread his seed in whatever barren field, whatever loveless sea? The Chirstians talk of sin and compile exhaustive lists, and list appropriate penalties. But sin is simply defined: causing gratuitous pain to men, animals, or plants."

"Tutelina," he shouted. "How many?"

"Nine, I think, my sweet."

"*Ten* for me."

"Hush! You will make me envious."

"If Dylan was born to sail, I was born to——"

"Enough," cried Stella. "We have fulfilled our bargain. The wind is rising. We must resume our voyage. For angry Christians are on our trail."

"Stella, so soon?" pleaded Tutelina. "I think I have missed one. See how mournful he looks?"

"Tutelina, for shame, you have lain with him twice at least."

"Have I, Stella? Must have lost count. My memory seems to be dimming along with my eyes."

The Sirens and Tritons, in great good humor, returned

to the sea and shoved their shoulders against the hull to help speed the ship on her way.

"Beware of Oceanus," Glaucus warned, "for he is a fearful god, and even we be afraid of his wrath and prefer the Inner Sea."

Somehow, unnoticed at first, one of the Sirens had managed to linger aboard the ship. No, she had only come when her sisters left, for she was a child and not a woman, with skinny shoulders and boyish thighs.

Nod did not catch a look at her face. But he noticed her silver wings and recognized Mara, even as clumsily—secretly, so she must have supposed—she sidled into the cabin where Dylan and Angus hid from the festival.

★ Chapter Four ★

"All those lovely forests and meadows. Oak trees big enough for a Dryad's house, and—what was that purple plant?"

"Heather."

"Heather. And you bring us here," sighed Tutelina. "Why, the trees are bent like Charon poling his barge. What few there *are*. Most are mere little bushes masquerading as trees. It looks like the coast where the slavers caught you. Caledonia, wasn't it?"

"*Is*," said Dylan, with terse finality. Stella had asked him to head for the place of his capture. Stella had asked him not to reveal her request.

"It must be our secret, Dylan."

"Keep a lot from me, girl." He wanted to add: "Been keepin' yourself from me too."

"More than I wish."

"Caledonia. Cold for a corn Sprite."

"Never mind. If I see it, I may be able to help you to remember."

"What?"

"Let's just say beginnings."

"Least I can make you a sealskin cloak."

"No, my dear. There may not be time."

"But the slavers got you once. Mightn't they come again?"

Stella hurried to answer for Dylan. "Remember, Dylan told us that this isn't their regular route. A storm blew them up here the time they captured him."

"Safer here than in the south," he added. "Romans all over the place down there. Londinium. Camulodunum. Some o' the folk are just like us. Worship the old gods. Some are Christian, though, buildin' basilicas 'stead o' temples. 'Sides, got Angus to help us. Haven't we, An-

gus?" The Telchin, who had pulled his weight throughout
the voyage and, on windless days, simultaneously rowed
six oars, nuzzled his head against Dylan's knee.

"We may be safe, but it certainly is cold, and it's still
summer," remarked Tutelina, borrowing warmth from
Nod with a movement which struck Dylan as an en-
gulfment more than a hug, and close to indecent,
doubtless because his Stella had lately been as parsimoni-
ous as a field mouse with a winter horde of grain. Perhaps
a sealskin would warm her heart. . . .

"Really, Dylan," said Nod. "You and I are men. But
you don't mean the ladies to make their home up here?
The sun looks downright bleached." Nod did not look
bleached. He had kept the bronze of the Italian sun, and
a man's muscles rippled under his skin. Every morning he
looked at his face in Tutelina's mirror, hoping to glimpse
the start of a beard.

Voices—fragments of memory—clattered in Dylan's
brain. He spoke loudly to hush the sound of them.

"Nay, lad. Visit my coracle, no more. Then find a
home in a forest south o' here but north o' the Romans.
Leastways, sea ain't rough today. We'll make for land and
beach the *Stella*."

They made for a promontory denuded of vegetation
but rank with sea-wrack such as broken shells, timbers,
fragments of granite, and decomposed fish.

"Coracle's close by."

"If the wind hasn't blown it away," said Tutelina. (It
was not her wont to complain at every step of the trip.
Usually laughter, a smile, at worst a sigh. But today her
mood reminded Dylan of how he felt when Stella kissed
his cheek instead of his mouth.) "Stella, can't you do
something with this stubborn male?"

"Would you keep a man from returning home? Dylan
is our captain. Besides, don't you want to see his coracle?
I do. It will remind us of Italia and our pilentum."

"Ah, yes," said Tutelina. "Remember those plush
couches and silken coverlits? Good for sleep. Good
for—"

"I remember," said Stella. "Many things. For what is a

man or a woman but memory laid upon memory, like many-colored bricks?"

"Those wi' poor foundations likely to crumble?"

"Not always, Dylan. You can build badly at first, but still raise a mighty tower. Or perhaps you have built well and simply forgotten."

He felt like a tower under siege. He did not even remember his mother.

Stella took his hand. He could feel her shivering in the frosty breeze and pulled her into the net of his embrace.

"Been cold to me, Stella," he chided. "Cold and far."

She clung to him with her old, yearning tenderness. He felt the frailty of her delicate bones. Somewhere, under the earth or on the sea, something had fled from her. He did not dare to give it a name.

"I know, my dearest. But the fault does not lie in you. Some of my memories cut like shards."

His flippered toes turned pink with desire and he released her before he could wreck the ship.

"Coracle's out o' the wind. We'll land and seek her out and build a fire. Nod, soon as I jump ashore, throw me a line. Angus, come wi' me. You can fasten a line the devil hisself can't loose." A lamentable slip of the tongue. He did not believe in the Christian devil. Only in devilish Christians.

The sight of his coracle made him want to cry. The paint had flaked from the hull. The mast, which had cracked in the wind, resembled the broken wing of an albatross, shredded of feathers.

"Never mind," said Stella. "Roanes have a gift for tidy houses, and you have friends to help. We'll soon make her clean and snug as a new pilentum."

At the touch of Dylan's hand, the hatch fell from its leathern hinges. A chill mist slapped his face. On deck and furnishings, on chest and chair and table, cobwebs and dust and salt lay as thick as a webbed foot. One wooden plate remained on the three-legged table, one dry fishbone, the single remnant of Dylan's last feast. They coughed in the dusty air.

Dylan opened a chest and removed a brush.

"Stick and broomweed," he said. "Made it myself." Soon he was wielding the brush like a sword and shouting orders in a captainly voice. "Nod, clean the table. Tutelina, fetch us some hammocks from the ship."

"But what are we going to eat?" she wailed. "One old fishbone?"

"Bring us some bread and cheese, and a *new* fish or two. Lots o' mackerel in this sea."

"I have never fished before," she confessed. "Generally, my lovers have seen to such needs."

"I'll do the fishing," said Nod with his usual gallantry. "You take a nap, Tutelina."

"Already got a job, lad. Tutelina hasn't. Learn, woman. Can't coddle you here in Caledonia."

Stella, without being asked, was stacking driftwood in the empty brazier.

"Tutelina," she said. "Bring us a lantern too." (Aboard the *Stella,* they kept a flame alight in a clay lamp, fed by oil, shielded from mischievous winds by a sheep's dried bladder.)

"Honestly. Caves haunted by demons. Pursuit by Romans. Rape at the hands of insatiable Tritons. And now this *servitude.* I am sure I have quite lost my color, to say nothing of my figure. Haven't I, Nod?"

"You haven't lost a single roundness, and you are as pink as a sweetheart rose. If anything, this northern air improves your complexion."

Mollified, Tutelina departed to perform her duties, though muttering under her breath, "Fish indeed! I will probably step on a crab and lose a toe."

"Angus, go wi' her," said Dylan. "*You* know how to fish." *Always had a pretty way wi' words, that Nod,* he thought. *True though about his lass lookin' good. Bicker like brother and sister, we do. But I love her right well, and there's a lot to love.*

Stella, not Tutelina, had lost her bloom. She resembled a holy virgin cloistered from the sun. Sacrificial: The ominous word was a wasp in Dylan's mind. Her fine cheek bones showed behind her translucent skin and gave her the wounding loveliness of Rahab or one of those other wingéd beings of ancient times. (In the Golden Age, it was said, the air was a single music of many wings. He did not welcome the thought of wings . . . flight . . . loss. Once she had been the fields. Now she was wrought of cloud, and clouds belonged to the sky.)

And so they cleaned the vessel and ate their bread and cheese, and the fish which Angus had caught, and they hung the additional hammocks from the *Stella*. Three weary people and one Telchin, warm, fed, comfortable, tumbled into the daffodils of sleep.

But sleep promised thorns instead of flowers to Dylan. He lay in a fretful waking and wondered why he fretted. He had come home. He had brought his friends. Ah, but Stella had left him in mystery. ("I may be able to help you to remember. . . .")

The hour-glass reversed its sands, time reeled backwards and tumbled him into a child. The place was the same and not the same. Somehow, younger. Cold, windswept, but truly home.

Coracles lay in rows along the beach, above the high-water mark and shielded behind a rampart of peat as tall as the tallest mast and topped with jagged thorns to discourage invaders. The town had been built to resemble a natural hill if seen from a ship at sea. Behind the wall, however, a happy people had built to suit their mood. The coracles were rainbows after a storm at sea, blue beside rhododendron-red, green next to daffodil-yellow, each of them flying a banner to match the hull.

Narrow cobblestone lanes divided the ships, and geraniums grew in baskets hung from the portholes cut in the hulls, and purple heather made gardens beloved by bees, a friendly defiance to the wind and the black basalt hills and the lonely cry of a curlew seeking a nest. Under the wall, a channel joined the village to the sea and allowed the Roanes to make their fishing trips or simply to swim and frolic and play their oceanic games. Sometimes the sealfolk swam the canal to visit the two-legged folk, and brought them the skins of their own dead for gifts—lucky skins—since a Roane would as soon kill a dolphin as a seal. Sometimes the sealfolk clambered onto the ground and waddled through the lanes, and the older Roanes could understand their language of yelps and barks (for those who have lost their youth may have gained a power which lies between wisdom and magic). A coral gate, like the mouth of a lobster box, could drop and close the canal against a flooding sea or invasion from Shelleycoats, who might discover the town which pretended to be a hill.

He ran along the seawall, laughing, to greet the return of his parents who had gone to fish in the sea. Slap, slap, slap went his webbed feet, and his heartbeat thumped in time. At eight, he was still too young for a sealskin around his shoulders, for the skin brought luck, and the children of Raones were thought to be lucky until they were men and women who had to fight against storms and sharks and Shelleycoats, snooping along the coast. Webfoot, his mother called him, proud of his sturdy webbed toes which shot him through the water with the speed of a seal. Pretty, translucent webs, each with its own small rainbow in the sun (a miniature of the town); strong webs, though, proof against rock or thorn. The feet he deserved, his mother said. "A bonny child, but strong enough for twelve instead of eight."

"Mama, Papa!" he called. His mother and father, rising in unison from the sea, net in hand, fish in net, each raised an arm to greet their son. They wore their nudity like a pride of robes: he with narrow thighs and a brawny chest developed by breathing both through gills and lungs, she with high, proud breasts and hair an ebony mist. What did they need to hide? Their cloaks covered only their shoulders, and not out of shame.

His father smiled a handsome, crooked-toothed smile. Once he had battled a shark to save his wife and broken a tooth in the tough, unyielding skin. His mother waved and he thought of faraway queens, wingéd and beautiful. Mo. Beautiful but not far; close at hand, loving him and his father (as if for them she had renounced her wings). They lived in a village of friends; they only needed the village of themselves.

"Webfoot, I brought you a conch," his father called. "You can whistle a dolphin to eat from your hand."

"And ride him across the sea and become his friend," said his mother.

"See," said his father, body wet and glistening in the sun. "I will call you a friend from the deep." For Roanes were affectionate folk. A father might kiss his son, whether bairn or boy or man; a friend might hug his friend. When a Roane gave his heart to a lass, he did not have to bind himself with laws; no other girl could fill his eye. Fidelity meant "I will" instead of "I must." Love was a single chest and not a set of tight little boxes, each with a different name, and some with locks. Nobody though of sin, except as indifference or cowardice or cruelty. (Yet the Christians of distant Rome had multiplied sins to fill a scroll! "Thou shalt not. . . ." The Roanes ignored the "not's" and hid when a Roman ship appeared in their waters. The wall of peat concealed their coracles.)

His father raised the conch shell to his lips. "See," he cried.

And he blew the shell.

But no dolphin answered the call.

Something slouched and rumbled out of the water, a procession of somethings in an undulation of waves: Green, matted fur, entangling sea-shells and the bones of fish and seals and—men? Lidless spider eyes. Flippers instead of fins or feet, slapping the sand with a hard but squishing sound.

The stench of them was worse than the look. He might have swallowed a rotten jellyfish, or a fiddler crab, pinching his nostrils, clawing and tumbling down his throat to lodge uneasily in his stomach. The sound of them was a shrill, whining laugh through the holes in their shaggy skulls. An upside down sort of laugh, he thought. Hate, not fun.

Shelleycoats.

"Go to your coracle, Webfoot," shouted a Roane, a bearded fellow wobbling on a cane. A giant clam had taken a foot.

"Mama and Papa. . . ."

"Canna help them now," said Hobbler, his kindly face contorted with fear and concern. "Come to attack the village. Never saw more than one at a time. *Must o' been sent.*"

Like a wall of slime, they thumped and slithered over the wall of peat, oblivious to its height or its cruelty of thorns. Eyes. Always, their yellow eyes, though almost hidden by fur, seemed to stare at Dylan and speak to him. "We have taken your parents. Now we have come for you."

They engulfed, they smothered, they smashed their way through the town. In place of heather and houses, they left a blanket of slime. And while they moved, they devoured. *He could hear the crunch of bones.*

Dylan stood his ground.

"Take me if you can, you old yellow beasties!" he shouted. No time now to hide in his coracle. None in which to hide! He stood with his people. He stood to avenge his parents. Nobody screamed or fled; Roanes were gentle but valorous folk. They liked to fish but they fought when they must, with building tools or the kick of their feet or a piece from a broken mast. They fought the living sea, but how could they win?

Dylan had been the first to lose. Still, he could fight. . . .

Abruptly he fell on his face against a cobblestone. Something—a flipper?—had struck him a glancing blow on his back. Then, as if he were swaying with currents under the sea, he felt himself lifted and carried before he slid down the trough of dream and battled night mares instead of day mares.

He awoke on a hillock above the village, behind a cluster of wild sea-grapes, their branches contorted away from the sea, their fruit eternally pale and hard and inedible. They might have been gnarled dwarves, frozen in flight. He could not discern the coracles or the Shelleycoats because of the plants. He knew the place. He had come here often to play and collect the arrow heads of an earlier folk. For the hillock had been a burial mound.

"They have gone, little Webfoot. All of them." A lady

whose face was suffused in mist had knelt beside him. Her
voice did not reveal her age. It was soft and kind, but she
might have been rich in years, or a young Roane lass of
an age to wed. Her robe was green, but its cloth was
strange to him.

"The Shelleycoats?"

"Yes. Returned to the sea. They only came to steal and
destroy."

"And Mama and Papa?"

"Returned to earth."

"Mean they're dead," he corrected. The Roanes lived
daily with life and death. They told their children stories
of love and valor; of poets and kings; they also told them
that Shelleycoats came from the sea, and murderous
storms, and slavers from the south. Dreamers, they still
knew the dream from the truth.

"Yes."

"Everybody? Hobbler too?"

"Yes."

He did not care about everybody. He did not care
about anybody except his parents. He must either talk or
cry.

"Got to be brave," he said. "Build back the town."

"Even my brave little Webfoot can't do that by himself.
There is nothing left but a ruin, and the wind will see to
that."

"Are you from the burial mound?"

"Yes."

"Are you a Shade?" Why could he not discern her features? Still, he sensed a smile.

"I am no more a Shade than you. Here. Feel my arms."
She hugged him, and her arms were soft but strong. She
smelled of heather and thyme.

"Will you help me, beautiful lady?"

"Yes, but not in the way you mean."

"Never mind. Don't want to build nothin'. Just want
to—"

What did he want? Cry. (His father had said: "To be a
man is to be unashamed of tears.")

He returned her hug; he made a nest of her arms and

pretended himself a fieldmouse, escaping a hawk. Nevertheless, his mother and father could build a better nest. Almost, he wanted the hawk to snatch him into the land of Shades.

"I will give you a gift," she said.

"Send me to Mama and Papa."

"It is I who must choose the gift. You see, I have work for you."

She sheltered him in a cave and salvaged a hammock from the ruined town. He already knew how to fish: She showed him the wild berries which grew in the seemingly barren hills, and a root, called camomile, which he could boil and make a drink.

"Goin' away?" he asked, with the knowledge which comes to children and madmen and the very old.

"Yes."

"Guess I need a sealskin now," he said. "Luck's goin', you see."

She brought him the skin and left him her final gift: Forgetfulness.

"Dearest Dylan," said Stella, kissing his cheek. "Were you having a nightmare? You were thrashing your arms, and there are tears in your eyes."

"Rememberin'," he said. "Said I would, didn't you?"

"Ah," she sighed. "That can be worse than a dream."

"Wasn't all sad."

"What wasn't, Dylan?" It was Nod.

"Tell you later, Nod." His voice was brusque.

Nod turned his face and made a cocoon of his hammock.

"Nod! Can't tell you now." Had he hurt his friend?

"Yes, Dylan?" Hopeful, still wanting to help.

"Wasn't all sad because it was a bridge. Canna tell you much, though. Canna see the end. Un'erstand?"

"Not exactly, Dylan, but you don't have to tell me."

"Can't. Bridge ain't finished yet. Met you. Met Stella. 'Spect I'm on the arch right now." He seized Nod's hand and drew their hammocks together and gave his friend a playful nip on the ear.

And Stella?

Her hand was cold.

As if she were going away.

He could not endure another goodbye. He leaped from his hammock and tried to hold her in place.

"I'm here, Dylan."

"Are you, Lass? To stay?"

"As long as I can."

"Long?"

"Little."

"Like the wind?"

"Yes."

And she sang a cruel song:

The windflower loves the wind
As an albatross the sea,
A marigold the morning sun,
And bergamot the bee:

The wind who spreads his bud
With a roving, girlish gust
And whispers him to sleep at night
In a bed of pollen dust.

The windflower loves the wind,
But does that wanderer care?
However she may whisper love,
Her heart is made of air.

"Don't like the wind. Fickle."

"She can't help herself."

"And you, Stella?"

"Her problem is forgetting too quickly. Mine is remembering too long. Still, we are both wanderers. She goes because she will. I go because I must."

"Guess I know what you mean. Almost."

"Do you, my dear? You are a wise boy."

"*Boy*?"

"I should have said man."

"Sure should've. Think a boy could—could—love you like I do?"

"I ought to wish that you loved me less. Ought, I say."

"Nay! Love me more and be proud. What'd you tell Nod's mother? 'Wi'out goodbyes, there canna be hellos.' "

He lifted her into his hammock, and love was a simple holding of hands and pressing of cheek to cheek, but Stella was beautiful and Dylan was proud.

Still, he did not like the wind.

★ Chapter Five ★

Nod was sad.

The treeless mounds of Caledonia dwindled into invisibility, like a school of whales in noble retreat. A barren land, to be sure, but he had been happy in Dylan's coracle and should have been happy hoisting sail. A sturdy deck, a stout captain, friends, and a light-o-love: Elysium above the ground. Was he not "merry Nod," always ready for sun, interludes or adventures?

Nevertheless, he was sad.

"Too late," he sighed.

"What's that you say, lad?" asked Dylan.

"Born too late. I don't care if I am a corn Sprite. I can't be happy all the time can I, Dylan. Not these days. It isn't exactly the Golden Age."

"Mackerel's best o' all the fish," said Dylan, thoughtful. "Sometime, though, bit o' octopus makes for a change. Know what I mean, Nod?"

"Roanes like seafood."

"Missed my point, lad. Don't have the Celtic gift o' fancy."

"Oh, I see what you mean. It's time for all of us to eat octopus for awhile. Of course I understand."

"Didn't always," said Dylan without reproof.

"I know. I always loved you though."

"You didn't, didn't you, Nod?" said Stella, looking so bodiless that the tiniest breeze might have wafted the soul from her lips. "You are a rare friend to Dylan. To love those we understand is a gift. To love without understanding is a miracle."

"Christians don't love us. Don't love *them*," said Dylan. "Hate 'em, in fact. Leastways, Walrus and Nod's old man."

141

"Of course you do, my dear. You still have bricks to lay, and so do I."

"Where're you leading us, Stella?" asked Nod. "Where're we going to lay all of those bricks?"

"Somewhere warm, I hope," announced Tutelina, huddling out of the breeze against the statue of Lordon, her bounties concealed beneath a sealskin cloak.

"To the Not-World, where else?"

"Dylan has told me about it," said Nod. "But he's never been there himself. Do you think it will be a happy place?"

"Never look for happiness, Nod. Simply be like a coracle warm with the heat of a brazier, table set for a feast, hammocks hung in a row. In time she will knock on your door, a stranger who may become your friend. When she chooses."

"Towers. Coracles. Stella, dear, I do wish you wouldn't wax philosophical," objected Tutelina. "You know I haven't a mind for such niceties."

"You have a mind for more than you know."

"Where's Angus?" inquired Nod. Angus was not a pet and not a servant; he was a friend. Homely, yes. Ugly, no. He ought to be with the crew.

"In the cabin," said Dylan. "Tendin' Cerberus' puppy. Put a live fish in the pot." An Adonis pot, black clay with red Rauns pursuing amenable nymphs to an inevitable conclusion. "Food, don't you see. Farmers use potash. Angus uses fish. Little critter already has six heads. Jove, how they eat! By the way, name's Argus. Angus named him after Ulysses' dog. Hound that knew him when he come home from Troy, lookin' like a beggar."

"Angus can't talk," said Nod. "How can he name a plant?"

"Beat out ARGUS wi' his feelers." To argue with Dylan when he was at the helm was like asking the rocks of Chrybdis not to clash.

"But he isn't a *real* dog," insisted Nod, remembering with alarm the time when Cerberus had almost devoured his friend. "He's a man-eating plant with six heads."

"*Dog*," said Dylan, brooking no argument. " 'Sides, he'll only eat who Angus or me says."

"Dylan, please don't look at me that way," said Tutelina, whose nearsighted eyes were sometimes conveniently sharp.

"When he's big, he'll be a lot to feed. You'd make him a tasty dish, Tutelina. All them hills and valleys. One big dessert. Stella's too skinny now. Nod's too tough."

"My geography," said Tutelina loftily, "is reserved for Nod. Except of course in the line of duty, as when I martyred myself, to borrow a Christian phrase, and appeased the rapacious Tritons."

"And Tutelina has spoiled me for anyone else," said Nod. "Except of course if we should be overrun by amorous Sirens."

Dylan looked wistful. His eyes held friendly seas. Was he remembering Mara, the Siren child, she who had doubtless summoned the Tritons and Sirens to the *Stella*'s defense?

With a prayer to the Tempestates, goddesses of the wind, they descended the western coast of Caledonia into a warmer climate. Storm-twisted bushes yielded to oak and elm; melancholy curlews to frolicsome puffins which sometimes perched on the deck and pecked crumbs from Tutelina's hand.

"Plump little critters," remarked Dylan. "See who they take to."

Argus, under the tending of his adoptive parent, Angus, grew with alarming speed, burst from his pot with a flurry of roots, and had to be planted in a cask on deck, under a canvas, and watered with wine. Fortunately his necks had grown so long that he could fish for his own dinner, dipping a head into the sea with the speed of a fisherman's spear and rising with a sturgeon or tuna which he carefully divided between the other heads, with the choicest morsels reserved for Angus, and even some leavings—a fin, an eye—for the rest of the crew. Otherwise, he would have exhausted the ship's provisions.

"What's it like, the Not-World?" asked Nod.

"Oh," said Dylan. "Fey."

"One of your Celtic words, no doubt. Give me a good Latin answer."

"Don't know."

"Stella?"

"Anticipation is a trickster. The truth is always better or worse."

To Nod, the answer was an obfuscation. He tried to read her face. He could as easily find an answer in the foam which enwreathed the ship, silver but evanescent.

They made for a narrow beach of gray sand and round pebbles—Britannia, not Caledonia. To the south lay Roman Exeter, a city of temples and churches, old gods and the new god: a city of risk for Roane and three Sprites. Slaver and Christian equally posed a threat. Here, so they hoped, was safety and secrecy.

There were dangerous shoals in the bay. Rocks broke the surface like the bodies of octopi. But the forested hills, lush with midsummer, were bountiful waterfalls which rustled liquidly in the wind and seemed to whisper, "Bathe in my torrents of leaves. Dive for secrets deeper than murex caves."

"Blackberry and fern and hawthorn," began Dylan. "And rowan and—"

"How can you possibly tell from such a distance?" asked Tutelina. "All I see is a series of lush green mounds. And I'm a fertility Sprite, though a trifle nearsighted, as you know."

"See *and* smell," he explained. "Animals too. Stag. Boar. Don't know the third. One horn on its head 'stead o' two."

"A unicorn?" asked Nod, who had never seen such a beast. "I thought they were extinct."

"Not here, lad."

"Indeed," said Tutelina. "Unicorns are said to be partial to women like me. I believe they nestle their heads in a lady's lap."

"Too late, Tutelina. Got to be a virgin."

"And then they guard her with their lives and serve her until they die." She had changed her cloak for a gossamer

gown like a light morning mist on her hills and valleys. At
any moment, it seemed, the mist might rise.

"We're safe," said Stella, smiling a strange, private
smile, as if returning to a familiar place, reluctant at first;
hesitant; at the last, however, resigned. "Not a Roman in
sight. Not a Christian. We'll beach our ship and—"

One of the rocks in the bay abruptly divided and pro-
jected its darker portion into the sea.

An evil secret.

A ship like a wooden shark, captained by men encased
in bronze.

Side by side stood two captains. Two executioners.

Marcus and Walrus.

They never reached the shore. The ship with the eyes
of a shark was as swift as the creature for which it was
named. There was time for questions but not for answers.
How had Marcus been rescued from drowning after the
Sirens and Tritons sank his ship? How had he met the
Walrus and known where to hide and lurk? Well, the
ways of the Desert King were as inscrutable as his coun-
tenance.

Now, flight:

Angus, furiously dipping an oar with each of his legs,
Dylan at the till, Tutelina seizing a seventh oar to break
the teeth of the *Shark,* and, strangely, comforting Stella,
who stood bemused, transfixed, useless among her ship's
defenders.

"Look to the ladies, Nod. No place to hide. . . ."

No place to hide . . . little wind . . . not enough rowers
to equal the speed of the *Shark.*

What is papyrus against a beak of iron? Feast, not defense. A crumpling hull . . . the sound of rushing waters
. . . Nod on the deck, Nod in the sea. . . .

The mast of the sunken *Stella* thrust from the water
like a flag of surrender.

The water was cold but not freezing; unlike some Roman boys, Nod could swim. He did not swim for the
shore; not at first. He swam in search of his love. An oar

floated past him, a gossamer robe—alas, devoid of Tutelina.

"Tutelina!" he yelled. She has already drowned, he thought. She was born to the fields and not the sea. Her bounteous curves will be a banquet for crabs. Spars floated past him, the wooden statue of Lordon. . . . Bonus Eventus without an arm.

"Here I am, Nod," she called, gliding toward him with strong, supple strokes. "Oh, my dear. I was so afraid for you. I didn't know if you knew how to swim!"

"You've lost your gown," he cried, for want of words to express the inexpressible. The truth was clear to him; his light-o-love had become his belovéd.

"I didn't lost it, I divested myself of it, the better to swim to *you*."

Her explanation was unarguable and admirable. Venus risen from the foam, he thought. Rubicund and delectable. (Under other circumstances, he mused. . . .)

"Where did you learn to swim?" she asked.

"In the river near Misna," he blubbered, spitting water and seaweed out of his mouth. "Barely. Dylan will be all right. He's a Roane and a sailor too. But Stella. What about her?"

"Stella can do anything. Almost."

"In her present state? She couldn't keep us from being rammed. And when we were, she looked so—lost."

"Never mind, it was just a mood. She has a way, you see."

It seemed to him that Stella had lost her way. Dylan would see to her, though, and six-legged Angus was clumsy but unsinkable.

"If we can just get to shore and join the others and climb the hill, they'll never find us. Sure you're all right, my sweetest?"

"I can't sink if I want to," she confessed. "You might say my mountains are permanent floats. Come, dear. We've escaped them before. Nod. NOD! I think an octopus has seized upon my extremities. Holy Ceres. He's lifting me out of the water."

"A net," groaned Nod. "It's got us both. We've been *fished*."

Tangled in the irresistible fibers of the net, they twisted and flailed and intermingled but felt themselves hoisted irrevocably aboard the *Shark*.

They tumbled out of the net and helped each other to an uncertain stand.

"The sailors are ogling me, Nod. Do something, my dear. I see rape in their eyes."

There was more than rape in the eyes of the sailors, long from their women, and of their officers, armed with spear or sword. Slavery or even murder awaited the victims. A slaving ship had become a man-o-war.

Stella and Dylan were scattered beside their friends. Nod could hardly rejoice in such a reunion. He wished the four of them into the sea.

"Well, caught us a Roane and three corn Sprites," Walrus leered. "Strange fish in these waters. Bring a handsome price, though!"

Marcus was smiling his slow and arrogant smile. Nod preferred his glare.

"Greetings, my son. We meet again. And for the last time, I trust." The scar on his brow gave a crooked cast to his eyes. He wore a breastplate and greaves, and he looked like a man in love with war, not for it's gains but its deaths.

"I thought you had drowned," spat Nod.

"Is this a Roman's celebrated filial piety?"

"I have a mother. I haven't a father."

"You have, haven't you? Sweet, simple Marcia. But as I was saying, I clung to the mast until Bibulus—stranger then—friend now—sailed to my rescue in *Shark*. (I believe you call him the Walrus. Inexcusable, to say the least.) How he happened to find me even he cannot explain. Something about a voice. In answer, I should imagine, to my prayers. He's a faithful Christian, of course. Then we came for you, and this time we followed a trail of foam by day, a pillar of fire at night. Anyway, here we are. Exeter lies to the south, and slaves are stripped and—"

"Lecherous," moaned Tutelina.

"And placed on a block and sold to the galleys."

"Or brothels," added Walrus. He bared his yellowing molars. His bristles quivered anticipation. He had the look of having been squashed.

"Salacious," wailed Tutelina.

"Of course your friend has already been an oarsman. You have always been quick to learn, however. And I see you've developed some muscles since we met in the cave. You may survive for a year or two in the galleys. Here now. The net is raising a further prize."

The prize was such a tangle of fibers and human limbs and vegetable necks that Nod mistook it at first for a portion of ocean floor.

"It's Angus clutching to Argus," said Tutelina, unblinking. "He's lost his cask. But see, his heads are waving manfully. Or should I say caninely."

"Why, I believe it's a seedling from my old friend Cerberus," said Marcus. "We shall have to root you again, child, and I have no doubt you'll grow as large as your mother and serve me as well. In fact, you haven't far to grow." Then to Angus, beam becoming glower: "But this—this six-legged beast. This Telchin. He bit my ankle in Dis's cave. It still gives me pain at times. Nobody wants such a freak, not even the circuses in the provinces."

Angus sprawled on the deck, legs collapsed, antennae wilted like waterless flowers. He made no attempt to rise. He had saved his friend and exhausted his strength. He looked from Dylan to Argus as if to say, "No more to give."

Marcus raised his sword and brandished it teasingly, tauntingly above the Telchin's neck.

"A quick blow to the head?" he mused. "It should roll like a coconut. Or one leg at a time. The slow way is best, I think. Let him repent at leisure."

The sword poised in the air and fell to the deck. Marcus followed the sword. Spreadeagled on the deck, he raised a hand for support and met a maw which lifted him from the planks and flung him into the sea, as a delicate lady may dispose of a mouse.

His armor made him a giant sinker. He sank with many bubbles and a single groan.

"Men, fish him out," cried Walrus. "You there. And you—"

It was his last order. Six heads smote him in unison.

He resembled a large ham encased in crumpled armor.

"Jump," cried Dylan.

They had reached the beach before the astounded crew could manage a single spear. Helping each other, Angus carrying Argus on his back, they started to climb the hill.

"Dylan," said Nod. "Have we really made it?"

"Hope so, lad."

"Stella?"

Stella was mute. She looked over her shoulder like— what was her name? Nod should remember from Marcus' lessons—Lot's wife, yearning for Sodom. She looked like a pillar of salt.

"I don't know," she said. "I only know that we are *between.*"

"Between what?" Mara had climbed from the sea and overtaken them on the side of the hill. She took Dylan's hand. "I followed you all the way," she said. "Do you mind?"

"Can't leave the sea, lass," he cried. "Said so yourself!"

"There'll always be streams or lakes. With you for a guide, I think I could climb Olympus."

"Stella's our guide."

"Am I?" she asked. "Yes, of course I am. Come then. We are expected."

★ Chapter Six ★

"Do you think that Marcus' men are hot on our trail?" asked Tutelina.

"Not to worry," said Dylan. "Kept a stiff pace. Proud o' you, Tutelina. With all your, er, geography, thought you'd hold us back."

"If anything's holding us back, it's your flippered feet," she replied, increasing her pace and navigating the path with the ease of a Siren in water.

Dylan smothered a smile. He had come to enjoy their little tiffs. Thus, he supposed, did sister and brother bicker and huff and love each other but never admit their love. "Mara, how 'bout you?"

The child had not complained of the long, swift climb from the sea, though Sirens rarely walked on the land and the lack of the steadying pressure of water caused her to stumble and lurch. In the steeper places, he quietly gave her a boost or a hand's support.

"Don't confuse me with Tritons," she said. "*I* have feet. Sometimes I walk for miles on the ocean floor."

"Homesick, Lassie?"

"I am with my friend," she said with quiet simplicity.

" 'Friends,' you mean."

"I said what I meant." In the time since she had helped him escape from his falley and guided him to the Styx, she had scarcely grown in height, but growth was evident in the way she walked, assured even if awkward; arms no longer akimbo like those of a child, but swaying in harmony with her body: except for her legs, one harmonious motion, even the silver hair and milky shoulders. She did not begin to fill Dylan's eye; to him she remained a child; still, he sensed the change.

At last they came to the foot of the tallest hill and the path exploded with rhododendrons.

"Such colors!" cried Tutelina. "Why, they put to shame our Italian poppies."

"They borrow their colors from Ceridwen," said Stella. "An old Celtic goddess. The red which is almost purple from her hair. The white from her flawless skin. She lived in a fountain, you see, and rarely saw the sun."

"It isn't really a hill, is it?" said Nod, ignoring the flowers and talk of goddesses. "It's a cliff disguising itself with vegetation. Ferns as tall as a woman. Moss as soft as a woman's hair. All the sharpnesses hidden or softened."

"Ferncliffe. And the path goes completely around it."

"And into—?"

"The Not-World."

It was then that they heard the song.

"Stella," cried Dylan. "Might be Orpheus playin' his lute. Lot o' lutes, for a fact. Never heard nothin' so sweet and pinin'."

"Your lutes are birds," she said. "Celtic nightingales. The goddess Ceridwen became a bird when her lover was killed by a boar. 'I will sing of my sorrow,' she said. 'But not without hope. For all things return in time.' And the birds you hear are descended from her."

"Stay in the Not-World, do they?"

"In the outer world, they think themselves plain, drag little things without any gift. In the Not-World, they know themselves beautiful in their song."

"Rest a mite," said Dylan. "Soon there'll be no stoppin' and no turnin' back, will there, Stella?"

"No, my dearest. No turning back. Here, even Orpheus could not look over his shoulder."

"Cold, Stella?" The day was warm but Stella shivered and seemed to dwindle and close, like a Humble-plant when touched by a clumsy foot.

"Can I be your cloak?" asked Dylan.

She took his hand and drew him into the eyrie of her arms and whispered in his ear. "You are my cloak and you are my sword. I have called you a boy. I should have called you a god."

"Stella, Stella," he chided. "Dinna say such things! Not

a god! Call me a sunflower, and you my sun. Nay. Sunflower's too sleekit. More like a thistle."

"If I could leave you one gift, it would be the truth of you, the courage, the beauty, the faith. But perhaps I love you the more because you think the less of yourself."

Leave him a gift? The "leave" was strangely chilling to one impervious to cold.

"*Rest*," he repeated loudly to his friends. "Got a piece to go." He clutched Stella's hand with desperate tenderness. He would *not* be left with a useless gift of words. He would stick to her like a thistle (but who can hold the sun?).

"And it's about time," sighed Tutelina. "The thought of a couch is irresistible."

"How about rhododendrons?" asked Nod as he tumbled her into the flowers and played with her hair and tickled her ear with a blade of grass. Angus, carrying Argus, a burden even for him, collapsed on the ground and, tenderly extricating himself from his friend, examined the flowers for a merle or a grouse to feed the multiple heads; in truth, he needed a flock.

Their rest was short.

A lady approached them through the flowers. Her gown was prickly with cockleburrs; her hair a plaything of boisterous winds. Had she come from the cliff instead of the path? The sun shone in Dylan's eyes and at first he could not distinguish her features, except her smile. Still, he was neither surprised nor alarmed. She belonged to the place.

"You the tutelary spirit?" he asked.

"Dylan, don't you remember me?"

"Marcia!"

"Mother!" cried Nod, as he leapt to his feet (and rolled Tutelina among the rhododendrons). He lifted her into a generous hug and kissed her on either cheek.

"How you have grown, my son! My boy has become a man."

"I'm still your boy."

"And my belovéd daughter."

"Daughter?" Blankly he stared at his mother, so quick to forsake him for—whom?

Stella escaped from Dylan's grasp—she who had hardly greeted Marcia in the cave at Misna—and knelt at Marcia's feet.

"Child, child, when have I asked for your worship?" She took Stella's hand and gathered her to her breast. "You have brought them to me just as I hoped," she said. "But you have given them your heart, my daughter."

"The heart is a halcyon bird," said Stella. "Who am I to build cages? You taught me that. But I have obeyed you and performed your task. With help. With the help of my friends."

"And have I demanded too much?"

"There was a time when you searched the world for me. Can I forget?"

"It is not repayment I ask."

"I served out of love."

"And well. And now we are one."

Dylan stared at Marcia and did not like what he saw or heard. A faintness of mist—had she brought it from the hill?—a certain slant of sun—they seemed to youthen her. He wanted her old and motherly; garbed in simple home-spun and gray of hair. Mother to Nod, not Stella. Stella belonged to him.

And now we are one . . . he had heard the voice in the cave at Misna. . . .

In Caledonia. . . .

He, a small boy. . . .

"Dylan, you're remembering, aren't you? Everything."

"It was you," he said. "Saved me from the Shelleycoats. Brought me food. Made me forget. Never let me see your face."

"It was I."

"Who *are* you, beautiful lady?"

"I am Stella's mother."

"Nod's too?" He did not want to deny a mother to Nod.

"Nod I found in the fields and loved like a son. But Stella is flesh of my flesh. To you she is "Stella" because she had led you like a star. To me she is as I named her, Proserpine."

"Can't fool me!" he cried. "Proserpine was a goddess. Mother was Ceres, the *Great* Mother. Ol' Dis—Pluto some call him—stole her into the Underworld, and Ceres searched and grieved, and spring got lost and the crops wouldn't grow. Jove hisself found the girl and took her back from his brother for half the year and found spring too."

"My dear, did you expect me to come in a chariot of fire or a column of gold? That was the way of Jove, my brother. His heart was kind, but his ways were—how shall I say?—a trifle Olympian. And they served him well with all of those mortal girls. I forget their names and their numbers. But I am the earth. An old lady with many sorrows and many laughters. How should I come to you except as Marcia, robed in simplicity and seeking her dearest children?"

Nod had started to cry. Silent tears, the kind that burn without relief. He looked like a little boy enduring a man's pain.

"You're going away," he said. "Forever. You've only come for Stella. And I must lose my mother. And Dylan—why don't you think of *him?* Stella's his jo!"

"I know, my Son. I know. But even a goddess cannot live as she would. For the God beyond the gods has decreed a plan, and I am a little part, even as you, and the whole is a mystery hidden within a mist. Remember, Nod, going is not forgetting. Look for me in the spring, which comes to this land with a frosty breath, but comes no less. Look for me in the humblest daisy in the smallest field."

"It's you I want. What do I care about spring and daisies?"

"I have had my time. I came with the Golden Age. The Age of Tin belongs to the Desert King. But I shall abide. And you, my children—you too, in your way. For I have gathered you here to escape his wrath. Soon you will be the last of your kind. Corn Sprites. Roane. Telchin. Siren. Cerberus' child, the fruit of my own beloved earth. The

Desert King is ruthless because he knows my power. He has slain my children and shut his ears to their cries. It was he, Dylan, who sent the Shelleycoats against your village in Caledonia. It was he who guided Marcus in his pursuit of you. His followers think that Sprites are demons, and he has summoned his own demoniac hordes—angels, they are called, golden and beautiful, but ruthless with spears and swords—to rid the earth of my children. They have dragged your brothers and sisters from their caves or fished them out of the sea. But here in the Not-World, you will be safe from him. For the old Celtic goddesses, Ceridwen and the rest, cloaked the place from all who would do them harm. And you shall live out your lives in the fashion of Sprites, more than men, less than gods, long-lived but not immortal. Die in your time, but come again, perhaps under different names. Die, and live, and die, and at the last . . . who can foresee the ultimate plan? Even the Desert King is not omniscient."

"Why did he turn on you, the loving mother?"

"He loved me once in his way, that proud and insolent god. (Men called me Ashtoreth then.) Alone in his treeless hills, he sent me gifts of fig and honey and milk; he summoned me to his couch. And I—I pitied him—but I would not come. For he was harsh. Jericho, Sodom, Gomorrah—their people were neither better nor worse than Romans or Celts or Saxons. But he smote them with thunderbolts when they placed him lower than me.

"He must have his way. He must have a bride; if not a goddess, a mortal girl named Mary, a virgin from Bethlehem."

" 'She will bear me a son to build my earthly kingdom,' he said. But the Christ-child grew to a man and hearkened to me, and his father averted his face and allowed an ignorant mob to seize and crucify his son. And Christ wept from his cross, "My father, why hast thou forsaken me?" And the love he had taught was turned into Law by Paul, that hater of women and woman's gentleness, and those who revered the Christ forgot the man. They looked to the sky and forgot to look at the earth. They worshipped a cross instead of a cornucopia. Soon they will rule the earth—conquer her, not befriend her—and lose a part of themselves, for they were born of the earth, and of me, the Mother."

"Evil men," spat Dylan.

"A few like Marcus. Most are simply lost. Wanderers in a moor with fitful candles. Mistaking will-o-the-wisps for inflexible laws."

"But you are a goddess," cried Nod. "And Stella too. How can goddesses live without any temples or priests?"

"Can men forget their mother? They will build churches in honor of Mary, but worship me. They will build chapels to saints—Cecilia, Theresa, maidens beyond number—but worship my daughter."

"But who am I?"

"When the power of the Desert King extended to Rome, I went among my people to see to their god. I was many women, mother and maiden, harlot and wife. At the last I was Marcia, wife to Marcus, of all the Christians the worst, the demon who looked like a man, the man who looked like a demon. I walked in the fields when Marcus sailed in his ship, and I searched for my threatened children to find them a home. I found Tutelina, one of the Old Ones. Did you know that she knew Aeneas?"

"Marcia, please. You make me sound like an agéd crone!"

"Years are what we learn. Boast of your years and Nod will love you the more!"

"I already do," said Nod. "I've always liked older women. But who on earth am I?"

"Once—I remember the sun like a gourd in the sky—I found a hole in the ground where a Roman wagon, carrying produce from the fields, had crushed and mangled the earth, and the earth had hidden your home, an underground cave. Your parents were dead. But you—in a tiny room, in a cradle made from a turtle shell—I found asleep and unharmed. The cradle had overturned and become your fort. Daily I brought you food and milk and talked to you in the wordless language of love. You laughed, and you made me laugh in that sorrowful time, and I named you Nod. Merry Nod.

"Then Marcus returned to see to his crops. I carried you into his own fields, and brought him to you and asked him to make you our son. He thought you would bring him gain. He let you live with us. I would have killed him if he had threatened you. The rest you know.

"But the time is at hand."

She raised her head and looked toward the face of the cliff, a ledge, an opening into the heart of the rock. A dark, slender man, robed in a wolfskin, beardless but neither young nor old, hair obsidian-black, slowly raised his hand. He seemed to stand in the stillness of a god, and in that power which, even in overthrow, is a pride and an exaltation.

Stella lifted her arms in the immemorial attitude of prayer.

"It is my lord," she said.

"The Dark Lord? One that ravished you?"

"And set me beside him in Hades and made me his queen and won my love."

"Love him, do you, Stella?"

"Yes. As you love the sea."

"Better than me?"

"How can I choose, my dear? The choice is made for me."

"He'll die in that hill, lass. Who'll worship him there?"

"Men will call him Satan and honor him in the night, though they misunderstand his heart."

"Cruel man, Stella?"

"No. A man without laughter. But just. And lonely."

"Canna let you go to him!"

"You must."

"Nay!"

"My mother can give you oblivion, as before."

Sadly he shook his head. "Had enough o' that. Rather remember in pain that lose the best o' myself."

"It is a happy place," said the Mother, "this Not-World of the Celts. You will build palaces out of timber and moss, and spend your days in merriment and your nights in love. Streams for a Roane and a Siren. Fields for fertility Sprites. Forests where unicorns mingle with deer."

"Nights o' love? Nod, maybe. Tutelina. Days too. Not me." Despair, like the Old Man of the Sea, seemed to straddle his shoulders.

"The heart is a murex shell. Its chambers are many, and who can foresee its windings?"

"Dylan." He had forgotten the child at his side. "I'm here."

"Mara, you're just a wee girl."

"I am almost fourteen," she said. "Why, I could be your wife!"

"I maun die wi'out Stella!"

"Give me your hand," said Stella.

"Cold, lass. Goin' to a cold place in the hill."

"Pretend that your mind is a casket wrought for jewels—or secrets. Carved from ivory to hold ebony. And this is my secret: 'We will meet again.' "

"When, Stella, when?"

"In a year or a thousand years."

He paused and struggled for words to bind her like tender chains.

"Guess I'll bide then. Want Argus and Angus wi' you? Knew Argus' mother, Cerberus, didn't you?"

"She guarded the Styx for me once."

"Yours then. Both. Can't separate 'em."

"Or them from you, my dear. They are my final gifts to you."

"Don't want a gift. Said so once. Want my Stella."

"I have given you half of my heart."

"Half's no better than a Shade, lass."

"Time is a kind friend, if you win his trust. And remember: What is hello without goodbye?"

And Tutelina sang, foolish, nearsighted Tutelina, wise with the wisdom of the Golden Age:

"I'll probably stumble," she said.

But she sang like a Celtic nightingale:

It is the time
Of Shades. They come
Not clamorous
With grief nor dumb
With loneliness,
But eloquent
With beating wings
And colors bent
To dapple me:
Kingfisher blue
And robin red
(The red is you).
It is the time
Of Shades, and I
Uplift my arms
As if to fly
Until the beating
Red and blue
Are hushed again
(And you, and you).

Acknowledgments

The Gods Abide is a novel, not a polemic against the Christianity of Constantine's day. Told from the viewpoint of the last demi-gods, my story naturally portrays the Christians in a garish light. It is a historical truth, however, that some of the Christians, once they came to power, treated the pagans with a ruthlessness worthy of Joshua leveling Jericho. For one of many such instances, read *Hypatia* by Charles Kingsley.

I confess to an inexcusable distortion of Celtic mythology. In the original myth, the goddess of Ceridwen transformed herself into a hen. Wanting my reference of her to sound poetic instead of culinary, however, I performed a further transformation: hen into nightingale. May my Roman gods protect me from Celtic wrath.

I am deeply indebted to Charles Leland's *Etruscan Magic and Occult Remedies*, a book which, solid enough for scholars, fanciful enough for dreamers, tells of pagan survivals in modern Italy (Nodotus and Tutelina are happily lodged among its pages).

For the geography, the flora, and the fauna of England and Scotland—Britannia and Caledonia in my story—I have relished the pages and pictures of *This England,* published by the National Geographic Society.

The poems are my own, either written expressly for the book or reprinted with the gracious permission of *Lyric* and Achille St. Onge, Publisher.